D0175860

KAT AND THE EMPEROR'S GIFT
by Emma Bradford

Kat and her aunt Jessie travel back to thirteenth-century China. In short order, they meet the explorer Marco Polo and the warrior-emperor Kublai Khan.

But not everyone welcomes the two travelers. Their arrival sets off a power struggle in the Khan's court. Caught in the middle is Kat's new friend, Princess Cocachin. It seems she's going to be forced to marry a man she fears.

Kat and Jessie must find a way to help the princess. And they must solve another problem. For the Khan has forbidden Marco to leave China. Yet Kat knows that the history books say he returned to Europe at this time.

It's up to Kat and Jessie to set things right. Otherwise, they may be guilty of changing the course of history!

STARDUST CLASSICS SERIES

KAT

Kat the Time Explorer

Stranded in Victorian England, Kat tries to locate the inventor who can restore her time machine and send her home.

Kat and the Emperor's Gift

In the court of Kublai Khan, Kat comes to the aid of a Mongolian princess who's facing a fearful future.

Kat and the Secrets of the Nile

At an archaeological dig in Egypt of 1892, Kat uncovers a plot to steal historical treasures—and blame an innocent man.

LAUREL

Laurel the Woodfairy

Laurel sets off into the gloomy Great Forest to track a new friend—who may have stolen the woodfairies' most precious possession.

Laurel and the Lost Treasure

In the dangerous Deeps, Laurel and her friends join a secretive dwarf in a hunt for treasure.

Laurel Rescues the Pixies

Laurel tries to save her pixie friends from a forest fire that could destroy their entire village.

ALISSA

Alissa, Princess of Arcadia

A strange old wizard helps Alissa solve a mysterious riddle and save her kingdom.

Alissa and the Castle Ghost

The princess hunts a ghost as she tries to right a long-ago injustice.

Alissa and the Dungeons of Grimrock

Alissa must free her wizard friend, Balin, after he's captured by an evil sorcerer.

Design and Art Direction by Vernon Thornblad

This book may be purchased in bulk at discounted rates for sales promotions, premiums, fundraising, or educational purposes. For more information, write the Special Sales Department at the address below or call 1-888-809-0608.

Just Pretend, Inc.
Attn: Special Sales Department
One Sundial Avenue, Suite 201
Manchester, NH 03103

Visit us online at www.justpretend.com

KAT
and the
Emperor's Gift

by Emma Bradford

Illustrations by Kazuhiko Sano
Spot Illustrations by Deb Hoeffner

Stardust
CLASSICS®

Just Pretend, Inc.
Attn: Publishing Division
One Sundial Avenue, Suite 201
Manchester, NH 03103

Stardust Classics is a registered trademark
of Just Pretend, Inc.

First Edition
Printed in Hong Kong
04 03 02 01 00 99   10 9 8 7 6 5 4 3 2

Publisher's Cataloging-in-Publication
(Provided by Quality Books, Inc.)

Bradford, Emma.
　　Kat and the emperor's gift / by Emma Bradford; illustrations by
Kazuhiko Sano; spot illustrations by Deb Hoeffner -- 1st ed.
　　p. cm. -- (Stardust classics. Kat; #2)

　　SUMMARY: Kat and Aunt Jessie time travel to thirteenth-century
China, where Kublai Khan has forbidden Marco Polo to leave the
country.

　　Preassigned LCCN: 98-65894
　　ISBN: 1-889514-19-5 (hardcover)
　　ISBN: 1-889514-20-9 (pbk.)

　　1. Time travel--Juvenile fiction. 2. Kublai Khan, 1216-1294--
Juvenile fiction. 3. Polo, Marco, 1254-1323?--Juvenile fiction.
4. China--History--Yuan dynasty, 1260-1368--Juvenile fiction.
I. Sano, Kazuhiko, 1952- II. Hoeffner, Deb. III. Title.
IV. Series.

PZ7.B7228Kb 1998　　　　　　　[Fic]
　　　　　　　　　　　　　　　　QBI98-682

Contents

CHAPTER ONE

The Explorers Meet

Even with her eyes still squeezed shut, Kat knew something had changed. Just minutes earlier, she'd been standing in a warm basement. Now she shivered in the bone-chilling cold.

Slowly Kat opened her eyes and looked around. She and her aunt were alone in a narrow alley that was bordered by wooden buildings. The scene was blurred by dancing flakes of white.

"Snow!" Kat exclaimed. "Jessie, it's snowing!"

"So I noticed," replied Jessie. She let go of the handle of the time machine and brushed snow from her cheeks.

"I wonder where we ended up this time," said Kat excitedly. She and Jessie had made trips back into the past before. Yet Kat never lost her sense of amazement about their adventures.

"And I wonder *when* we ended up," added Jessie with a smile.

Jessie removed two medallions from the open drawer at the side of the time machine. Then she folded the legs of the device and placed it in the velvet bag at her feet.

"Here," said Jessie, handing Kat one medallion. "Let's put these on for safekeeping."

Kat slipped the golden chain over her head. Jessie did the

1

same with the silvery one. The medallions helped power the time machine, so they always guarded them carefully.

With that done, Kat and Jessie stopped to study each other. As on every trip, their clothing had changed. In their own time, they had been dressed in jeans, T-shirts, and sneakers. Now they wore beautiful coats and leather boots.

"I'd say that we've gone way back this time," said Jessie. "Our clothing looks like something from the Middle Ages."

"I bet you're right," commented Kat. "What about your bag, Jessie?"

She pointed at the velvet bag where Jessie had stored the time machine. The bag was one of the many mysteries involved in time traveling. Anything inside remained the same, no matter where they went. However, everything else— whatever they wore or carried—changed to match the time and place. That included the outside of the bag too.

Now Jessie looked inside. "The history encyclopedia is here," she reported.

"What about the camera?" Kat asked.

"It's here too," replied Jessie. She frowned as she held up a small instant camera.

Kat read her aunt's mind. "I'll be careful that no one spots it, Jessie." Both of them were worried about doing something that might change history. "I just want to see if we can take pictures back with us."

"I know," murmured Jessie. "But it makes me nervous having something so modern along. Who knows what might happen if someone notices it." She handed the camera to Kat. "This was your idea. So it's also your responsibility."

Kat grinned. "I'll put it in here," she said. She lifted the woolen bag that hung from her shoulder. "I guess this is what my backpack turned into this trip."

Jessie picked up her bag and led the way down the alley. In the bitter cold, the snow beneath their feet crunched like broken glass.

The alley came to an end at a stone-paved street. Kat and Jessie stepped forward and looked around. The street stretched out wide and straight in a seemingly endless line. Along both sides of the roadway stood sturdy wooden buildings. Fine carvings decorated the walls, while the tiled roofs curved up at the corners. And there were people everywhere.

"I've never seen anything like this," breathed Kat.

Puzzled, Jessie shook her head. "Neither have I—except in books. But from the look of things, I'd guess we're in Asia."

Kat's eyes moved from the buildings to the passersby. They were all bundled into thick coats or robes. And all were hurrying about their business.

It didn't take long for Kat to notice that those who caught sight of her seemed surprised. Their eyes would widen, then quickly drop from hers to the ground. They didn't appear unfriendly—just uncertain.

Kat and Jessie joined the crowd, walking slowly down the street. To their left, a door opened, and a blast of warm air flowed out. With it came the sound of a cheerful voice.

"I will have some more fine silks next week. The finest in all of Ta-tu! Be sure to come back!"

A man carrying a package hurried out the door. He gave Jessie and Kat a curious look before heading off.

"These buildings must be shops," said Kat. She looked at her aunt. "You understood him too, didn't you?"

Jessie nodded. "Yes. Though I haven't a clue about what language he spoke."

She sighed. She didn't mind not knowing what language she could suddenly understand. What bothered Jessie was not knowing how the time machine allowed her to do such a wonderful thing.

"I wish we didn't always forget every word as soon as we got back home," said Kat. "And it would be nice if we could read and write these languages too," she added. "At least while we're time traveling somewhere."

Kat pointed to a sign on a nearby building. "That looks like Chinese or Japanese writing. But I don't have any idea what it says."

"Let's go inside," suggested Jessie. "Maybe we can find out where we are."

They rang the bell. At once a short, smiling man opened the door. For a moment, he looked startled. Then he bowed and motioned them inside. "Come in! Come in! Step out of the cold!"

Kat and Jessie happily entered the warmth of the shop. They stopped and stared in delight as they took in the richness around them. Rolls of lovely fabric rose in stacks almost to the ceiling.

In a far corner, a tall man stood with his back to them. He thoughtfully stroked a length of red silk.

The merchant studied Kat and Jessie—especially Kat's blond hair and blue eyes. "You must be visitors," he said. "Welcome to Ta-tu."

Kat nodded, and Jessie answered quietly, "Thank you."

At the sound of Jessie's voice, the other customer turned and looked at them. "You are from the West!" he exclaimed. His bearded face broke into a huge smile, and he hurried across the room.

Kat and Jessie smiled too. The speaker was obviously a European—the first they'd seen.

"This is truly amazing," the man continued. "Astounding, in fact! I had thought my father, my uncle, and I were the only Europeans in these parts. But here you are! And women as well! May I ask what brings you here?"

Jessie and Kat felt tongue-tied. What could they say? They didn't even know where "here" was yet.

Fortunately the stranger was so excited that he went on to answer his own question. "You must be fellow explorers! Who would have thought such a thing!" He beamed at them happily.

"Yes," said Jessie. "We are explorers."

That's an honest answer, thought Kat.

"Women explorers!" marveled the man. "Where are you from?"

This time Kat answered. "Winchester," she replied, naming the town where they lived. She held her breath. With any luck, the man wouldn't find her answer suspicious. After all, she couldn't very well say they were from America. She felt sure they'd gone back to a time before Europeans had settled there.

"Winchester..." echoed the man. "Ah! Winchester, England!" Kat and Jessie traded relieved looks, grateful that such a place existed at this time.

The man smiled and went on without waiting for a reply. "Why, that is even farther away than my home—Venice!" Then he glanced around. "Where is the rest of your party?"

"Party?" echoed Kat weakly.

"We're not with any party," added Jessie.

"What!" exclaimed the man with surprise. "You came all this way alone? Surely not on such a long and dangerous trip!"

When Kat and Jessie didn't respond, the man gave them a knowing look. "Ah," he said. "I have seen this happen before to travelers. My guess is that your guides turned out to be thieves. They left you?"

Kat and Jessie just lowered their heads.

"How terrible!" the man exclaimed. "Well, I understand if you would rather not talk about it. But where are you staying here in Ta-tu?"

"We don't have a place to stay," said Jessie.

"And did the thieves take all your belongings?" he asked.

"We have nothing except these two bags," answered Kat.

"Two bags!" repeated the man. He shook his head, then smiled. "Let me set your worries to rest. I shall take care of things for you." With a bow, he added, "My name is Marco Polo. And I am at your service."

Kat and Jessie stared at him in astonishment. They were talking to Marco Polo, the famous explorer! It took Jessie a moment to gather her wits and introduce herself and her niece.

Polo bowed once more. "Lady Jessica and Katherine," he announced with satisfaction. "I am delighted to meet you.

"It will be an honor to assist you," he continued. "Just give me a moment to finish my business with this merchant."

He turned back to the shopkeeper. While the two talked of prices, Kat and Jessie moved to the far side of the shop.

"Marco Polo!" whispered Kat. "He lived a long time ago."

"I know," replied Jessie. She searched through her bag for the encyclopedia. With a glance to be sure the men were busy, she thumbed through the book.

"It says here that he lived from about 1254 to 1324. He wrote a famous book about his travels. And he spent a lot of time in China."

"But are we in China?" asked Kat. "I've never heard of a Chinese city called Ta-tu."

Jessie turned more pages. "Here it is. That's what Beijing was called a long time ago."

"So we're in China for sure," said Kat. She'd been keeping an eye on Marco Polo, and she saw him bow to the storekeeper. "Better put that away, Jessie," she said. "I think they're done talking."

Jessie had safely repacked the book by the time Marco Polo rejoined them. "Now if you will come with me, there is someone you must meet," he said. He pushed open the door and led Kat and Jessie into the street.

"Who is that?" asked Kat.

"The great Kublai Khan," he announced. "The emperor of all China."

CHAPTER TWO

The Emperor's Invitation

Kat gave Jessie a wide-eyed look. Kublai Khan! She tried to remember what she'd learned about him. She knew he'd been a powerful ruler. And that he'd controlled a large part of Asia. That frightened her a bit. What if the Khan wasn't as friendly as Marco Polo?

However, Marco didn't seem to doubt that they would be warmly welcomed. "The Khan is a very wise, very curious man," he told them. "He will be most interested in talking to other visitors from Europe. I am expected back at court now. So this is a perfect time to take you there."

Marco went on to explain that he, his father, and his uncle had been in China for nearly 17 years.

"Seventeen years!" Kat exclaimed. Marco Polo didn't look very old. He must have been away from home for almost half his life! "What have you been doing here all that time?" she asked.

Marco laughed. "Perhaps it would be easier to tell you what I have *not* been doing. My first purpose in coming here was to help my father and uncle. They are merchants and came to China to trade. In fact, this is their second trip. But I must be honest. I wanted to come because of my curiosity about China and the other lands of the East. And what I have seen has more than satisfied me. It is truly amazing."

As they walked, Polo shared tales of his journeys. He'd had many exciting experiences on the way to Ta-tu. And since his arrival, he'd traveled all over China, working on the emperor's behalf.

Kat hung on every word. Marco was a natural storyteller. His eyes sparkled as he created pictures in the air with his hands. And as he'd promised, his adventures were remarkable.

All too soon, Marco wound up his tale. "There is much more I could tell you about the wonders I have seen. But that will have to wait. We are almost at the palace."

He led the way around a corner and onto a wide street. Kat gasped at the sight of the huge walls that towered over their heads. She guessed that the walls stood at least 20 feet high and stretched a mile in each direction. Atop the corners, guard towers perched like crow's nests on ships.

Marco led them to a large gate in one of the walls. Almost every inch of the gateway was decorated. It was capped by a red tile roof with two carved dragons at the top. Marco explained that this was the entrance to the Inner City, where the palace of the Khan stood.

At either side of the gate were watchful guards. Their dark eyes seemed to drill into Kat. However, they made no move to stop Marco as he led his guests through the opening. It was plain that he was a common sight.

But Jessie was nervous. "I'm not sure what we're getting into, Kat," she whispered. "So stay close to me until we know what's going on."

Kat knew that Jessie worried about taking her along on time-travel trips. For one thing, Jessie didn't understand how the time machine worked. She had discovered it in the basement of the old house she'd inherited. The house and all its contents used to belong to Malcolm Adams, Jessie's great-uncle. Malcolm had started building the machine, but he'd never finished it. With the help of his notes, Jessie and Kat completed the work.

Jessie felt a special responsibility toward her ten-year-old niece. In a way, she was serving as Kat's parent. Kat's mother and father were gone for a year, studying plants in the Amazon. So Kat was living with Jessie, her mother's younger sister.

Kat, however, didn't share Jessie's concern. As usual, curiosity overcame any fears she might have. She gazed around in wonder as they entered a huge park that lay within the walls of the city. A frosting of snow covered the bare trees. In the distance, Kat saw a frozen lake.

They followed a paved path through the park. Passing beneath another gateway, they found themselves before an enormous building.

"Here it is—the palace of Kublai Khan," announced Marco Polo.

11

The sight took Kat's breath away. The painted roof shone like a rainbow of jewels—bright blue, yellow, green, and red. Surrounding the palace were many smaller buildings, just as lovely. A narrow terrace of marble formed a walkway around and between the buildings.

"It's beautiful!" exclaimed Kat.

"Unbelievable!" added Jessie.

"You will be just as pleased by what lies inside," said Marco with a smile. "Come!"

He led them up a marble stairway and down a long arched hallway. Finally he came to a halt in the grandest room Kat had ever seen.

"This is Kublai Khan's reception hall," he explained.

Kat's eyes went to the great domed roof. It was covered with images of dragons, birds, and other animals. Then she noticed that the room was filled with richly dressed men and women—hundreds of them. Some were talking in small groups. Others were listening to musicians, watching entertainers, or busily hurrying about.

"As you may note," began Marco, "the Khan entertains visitors from many faraway places. Though few come from as far away as you have," he added.

Marco pointed at two older men on the other side of the room. "My father and uncle," he said. "They have just returned from trading in the south. I would like you to meet them."

Marco led them across the room to make the introductions. The two men were both surprised and pleased to see Jessie and Kat.

After talking briefly with the Polos, Kat and Jessie turned to study the hall. Marco began to point out things of interest. "There are quite a few women here," observed Jessie.

"Many of them are the Khan's wives," explained Marco. "And his sons' wives."

Marco's words startled Kat. She wondered exactly how many wives the Khan and his sons each had. But she decided it wouldn't be polite to ask.

As he stepped back to let a small group pass, Marco smiled. "The court is more crowded than usual. You see, you have arrived at a very special time. In just a few days, we will celebrate the New Year. It is the greatest feast day of all. Many visitors are here to honor the Khan."

"Where is the Khan?" asked Jessie.

"Follow me. I will present you to him," said Marco.

He led them toward a man who was dressed in a robe of gold. The Khan didn't seem much like a warrior to Kat. Not only was he old, but he was short and heavyset. Yet as she looked closer, she noted the Khan's back was straight. And she saw that his dark eyes seemed to miss nothing.

A crowd of people surrounded the Khan, but two men were especially noticeable. Wearing robes of black and white, they stood one at either side of the emperor. The man on the left was gray-haired. Tall and lean, he had a long beard and full mustache. The dark-haired man on the right was younger and shorter. At the moment, he was speaking quietly into the Khan's ear.

"Who are those two men with the Khan?" asked Jessie.

"They are the chief astrologers of the court," answered Marco. "Very wise men who know much about the heavens. The Khan often seeks their advice."

He continued, "The older one is from Persia and is called Majeed. The other is Sung. He is Chinese. Now, if you will wait here, I will introduce you."

With that, Marco stepped before the Khan. The emperor turned away from his astrologers and nodded. "Welcome, Marco," he said in a ringing voice. "Did you succeed in your task?"

"I did, my lord," said Marco with a deep bow. "The cloth will be delivered later today."

Then he announced, "I made a discovery while at the cloth merchant's. You have visitors from England, my lord. Let me introduce Lady Jessica of Winchester and her niece, Katherine."

Kat and Jessie moved forward to stand beside Marco. Both bowed, just as they had seen Marco do.

The Khan's eyes brightened. But Sung's reaction was even stronger. At Marco's introduction, the Chinese astrologer's head had snapped up in surprise. Although he remained silent, he studied Kat and Jessie with a look of satisfaction.

Gray-bearded Majeed, on the other hand, peered at the visitors with distrust.

The Khan motioned Sung to step closer. "So, Sung, what have you to say about our visitors?"

The young astrologer didn't bother to hide his pride. "The truth of my vision has been revealed, your highness."

Out of the corner of her eye, Kat noted Marco's look of surprise. But the Khan merely nodded. Addressing Kat and Jessie, he said, "Your visit has been expected. You are most welcome here."

Expected? What in the world could the Khan mean? thought Kat.

Jessie merely replied, "Thank you, my lord."

The Khan's face lit up. "You speak my language," he marveled. His eyes traveled to Kat. "Do you speak Mongolian as well, child?"

"Yes, my lord," answered Kat. She smiled widely. It was hard not to share the emperor's enthusiasm.

"Splendid!" exclaimed the Khan. "Then you can tell me yourselves what strange and unusual wisdom you bring to my court."

"Wisdom, your majesty?" asked Jessie.

"Yes," replied the Khan. "Every visitor has his—or her—own wisdom. And I want to collect as much of it as possible before I die. So what do you bring?"

"I have some knowledge of the heavens, your highness," said Jessie. Her aunt spoke the truth, Kat realized. Jessie was a scientist, and she did know a great deal about the stars and planets.

"Excellent!" exclaimed the Khan. "I am sure you will have much to teach my astrologers."

He gave his attention to Kat. "Now, child, what can you offer?"

Kat gulped and stared into the Khan's lively eyes. His expression was one she'd seen in her own mirror—equal parts curiosity and wonder.

"I am young, my lord," she said softly. "So my search for wisdom is just beginning."

From the Khan's smile, Kat guessed that her answer pleased him. "I am old," he replied. "Yet in many ways, my search has also only begun."

He continued, "You will both stay here in the palace." Then he clapped his hands and called out, "Chin!"

A lovely girl with shiny black hair and gentle eyes stepped forward. To Kat, she appeared to be in her late teens.

The girl bowed low before the emperor. When she stood upright again, she gave Kat a warm smile.

"Princess Cocachin will help you learn about my court," said the Khan. "In return, I would like you to share the wisdom of England with her."

"I would be happy to tell her what I know, your highness," said Kat.

The Khan clapped his hands once again. "Sung! Majeed!" he barked. The two astrologers rushed to his side.

The Khan nodded to Jessie. "Sung and Majeed will take you to meet with the other astrologers."

Jessie and Kat exchanged uneasy looks. They didn't want to be separated. But it hardly seemed wise to object to the decision of an emperor. It was obvious that the Khan's requests were actually orders. And that he was used to being obeyed instantly.

The Khan turned back to Marco and began asking questions. Kat realized that he was done speaking to them.

A gentle hand touched Kat's sleeve. "Come with me, Katherine," Princess Cocachin said. "I will show you to your room."

Jessie handed Kat the velvet bag she'd been carrying. Then Kat followed the princess to the doorway. Jessie and the two astrologers came along behind them.

As Kat stepped into the hall, she stopped to say good-bye to Jessie. But the words died in her throat when she caught sight of Majeed's face. The old astrologer was staring at Jessie, his eyes burning with anger.

He doesn't want us here, Kat suddenly realized. I wonder why?

CHAPTER THREE

The Marriage of a Princess

I will tell you about the Khan's palace as we go, Katherine," said the princess in a soft, musical voice. Her silk gown swirled and swished as she walked along.

"Thank you, Princess Cocachin," replied Kat.

The princess laughed. "Oh, please, call me Chin. I would like us to be friends."

"I'd like that too," said Kat. "But then you must call me Kat."

"Very well—Kat."

They made their way past room after room. Kat listened carefully as Chin described everything. Before long she realized that the palace was actually a group of connected buildings. Kat also realized that without Chin she'd be hopelessly lost.

Kat noticed several rooms with guarded doors. Chin explained that the Khan's treasures of gold, silver, and jewels were stored there.

She also told Kat that a whole section of the palace was for the emperor's wives and sons. When Kat asked how many wives the Khan had, Chin admitted that even she didn't know.

"And this area is for the Khan's special guests," announced Chin at last. "Most visitors from other lands find rooms on the outskirts of the city. It is a great honor to be invited to stay here in the palace."

She stopped in front of an open door. "This is where you and Lady Jessica will be sleeping."

Kat followed Chin into the chamber. It was bigger than her bedroom in Jessie's house. Like most of the rooms in the palace, it featured carved and painted woodwork. A large dressing screen decorated with a mountain scene stood in one corner. The room also held a pair of square stools and two low beds with red silk covers. On the far wall was a set of doors. Chin explained that these led outside to a terrace.

As Kat looked around, Chin stepped out into the hall and clapped her hands. Two servants appeared. At Chin's orders, both of them left. They soon reappeared, however—carrying a large chest.

Beckoning to Kat, Chin lifted the lid. Kat gasped at the sight of the marvelous clothes inside. "Oh, Chin! These are beautiful!"

"Marco said that your guides took your belongings," said Chin. "I hope you and Lady Jessica will accept these simple gifts from me."

"They're hardly simple," replied Kat. "These are the loveliest clothes I've ever seen! Thank you."

Chin reached into the trunk and pulled out a white gown. "You must wear this at the New Year feast," she said. "Everyone dresses in white on the New Year. It is our custom."

Kat nodded but said nothing. The New Year was several

days away. She wasn't sure that she and Jessie would still be here by then. But she didn't want to say anything to Chin about that possibility.

Chin closed the trunk. "There is a bath down the hall," she said. "Let me show you the way."

Kat followed Chin to a nearby room, where she found a steaming pool.

"The bath water is heated by burning coal," said Chin proudly. "I know that must seem strange to you. Marco told me that he has never seen such a thing. 'Rock that burns,' he calls it."

They returned to Kat and Jessie's room. By now it was late in the afternoon. "I will see that Lady Jessica knows where to find you," Chin said. "And I am sure you are tired from your long journey. So I will have dinner brought to you here. But there will be great banquets for the New Year. Then we will feast together."

"Thank you," said Kat. "You've certainly made us feel very welcome."

"I am only sorry that it was too cold to show you the palace grounds," said Chin. "We will do that tomorrow."

"Won't it still be cold?" asked Kat.

"No," said Chin. "The Khan has decided that he is bored with cold weather. He told his astrologers he wants tomorrow to be a sunny, pleasant day."

Can Chin really believe such a thing is possible? Kat wondered. But she held her tongue. She reminded herself that she was far from her own time. Perhaps Chin would find TV weather reports just as unbelievable.

"I'll look forward to seeing the grounds when it's warmer," Kat said. "From what I've seen so far, Ta-tu is very beautiful."

"It is, is it not?" said Chin, with a trace of sadness. "I will miss it very much."

"You're going away?" asked Kat.

"Yes," said Chin. "I will soon be leaving to marry Argon, ruler of Persia."

"Oh," said Kat with some surprise. Chin was so young— surely only 16 or 17. But Kat knew that in times past, girls married early. So she only said, "I hope you'll be very happy."

"I am looking forward to meeting him," Chin replied.

Kat nearly choked on this information. "You've never even met him?" she asked in disbelief.

"No. But the great Khan wishes me to marry Argon. So it will be done." She smiled and bowed to Kat. "I will leave you now to rest."

Alone, Kat hid the velvet bag—with the time machine inside—at the bottom of the chest. Then she spent some time looking through all the wonderful clothing. But she couldn't stop thinking about Chin's upcoming marriage. Why should the princess leave Ta-tu and marry a total stranger? It didn't seem right—even for the thirteenth century.

Soon a servant appeared with Jessie. Kat eagerly showed her aunt around the guest quarters. The tour ended with the arrival of their dinner.

As they ate the meal of meat and spicy rice, Jessie told about her afternoon. "It's pretty amazing," she said. "The Khan must have thousands of astrologers—and they're from so many different countries! Needless to say, they don't all agree. Especially Majeed and Sung."

"The two who were in court earlier today?" asked Kat.

"Right. They both seem to have their own followers among the other astrologers. And then there's this 'vision'

Sung had of our coming. It seems to have created a problem between the two groups."

"What do you mean?" asked Kat.

"I'm not sure," replied Jessie. "Sung was strutting around, looking like he'd just won a prize. And when Majeed wasn't frowning at me, he was snorting at Sung. I decided it might be smarter not to bring up the subject."

"I saw Majeed giving you nasty looks earlier," noted Kat. "Somehow we've gotten on his bad side."

"I think it's safest just to keep my mouth shut," said Jessie. "Anyway, I don't want to change history by telling them something they don't know about the skies."

She sighed and added, "Still, it was an interesting experience. There's so much that they *do* know. In fact, I think they probably know far more than anybody does in Europe during this time. I only wish I could have seen their observatory. It's along the eastern wall of the city. But they won't take me there when it's so cold."

"Chin said that the astrologers are supposed to take care of that," laughed Kat.

"Yes. Today Majeed and some of the others were hard at work calling up warmer weather. They were looking for signs, chanting, and singing. I joined in myself."

"You didn't!" exclaimed Kat.

Jessie shrugged. "I didn't want to act as though I doubted their abilities. Besides, what's the harm in taking part? We're here to learn about this time and place, after all."

"That reminds me—I want to check something," said Kat. She opened the trunk, found Jessie's bag, and took out the encyclopedia.

"What are you looking for?" asked Jessie.

"I want to see whether the encyclopedia says anything about Chin. I'd like to know what happens to her."

Kat quickly leafed through the book, then sighed. "There's nothing in here."

"You sound upset," commented Jessie. "What's bothering you?"

"It's just that there are some things I don't like about this place," said Kat. "The idea of the Khan having so many wives is strange. But that's not the worst thing, Jessie."

She went on to tell her aunt what Chin had said. "Imagine having to marry someone you've never even met," she added. "To go thousands of miles away and never see your home again. And just because someone tells you to do it."

"You're thinking of how *you'd* feel," said Jessie. "Does Chin seem unhappy about the marriage?"

"Not really. But Jessie, don't you think she should mind?"

"I don't know," said Jessie. "I'm not a thirteenth-century princess. Things are very different here."

"I guess," Kat replied. Still, she couldn't help believing that a decision about marriage should be Chin's—and Chin's alone.

❧

The next morning, Kat and Jessie were awakened by the arrival of a young serving maid. The girl chattered nonstop as she set out their breakfast. She obviously enjoyed meeting two such unusual visitors.

After the maid left, Kat and Jessie sat down to eat. They also discussed what Kat had read the evening before. She'd checked the encyclopedia for information about the Khan.

"I was confused," she admitted to Jessie. "I knew Kublai

Khan was Mongolian. So I wasn't sure how he got to be emperor of China—a completely different country. The encyclopedia says his grandfather, Genghis Khan, conquered much of China. Kublai took over even more territory. And this was where he wanted to live. He really admired the Chinese."

By the time Kat and Jessie finished, Chin had arrived. Today she wasn't dressed in a fine gown. Instead, she wore a long, loose-fitting tunic over wide-legged pants. Her hair was tied back with a thin ribbon.

"Good morning," the princess said. She crossed the room and opened the doors that led outside. "The astrologers have given us a beautiful day," she observed. "Just as the Khan requested."

To Kat's surprise, Chin was right. Snow still covered the ground, but the sun was shining. The paved paths were clear, and the icicles that hung from the roof dripped steadily.

"When you are ready, Kat, I will show you around the palace gardens," said Chin. She closed the doors again.

"Will Marco be joining us?" asked Kat. She looked forward to seeing the explorer again.

"No," replied Chin. "The Khan has sent him on an errand. There is much to do with the New Year celebration only days away. But he will be back tomorrow."

Jessie joined them at the outer doors. "I'd love to tour the gardens too," she said.

"You shall have a chance to do so, of course," responded Chin. "But not today. The Khan has different plans for you."

Jessie nodded. For a moment, Kat thought she saw a flash of worry in her aunt's eyes.

"Do you know what the Khan wants Jessie to do?" asked Kat.

"No," replied Chin. She seemed surprised to be asked such a question. "It will be explained, I am sure."

Jessie gave a small smile. "We'll get dressed," she told Chin. "Should Kat wear an outfit like yours?"

Chin smiled. "Yes, that would be best." At the door, she turned back to Kat. "When I return, I will bring a surprise."

Kat and Jessie rooted through the trunk to find something to wear. Jessie chose a gown of blue and pink silk. Kat found loose pants and a tunic like Chin's.

When they were both dressed, Kat opened the door that led outside. She stood and gazed at the sunlit park. "Maybe those astrologers know something we don't," she said with a shake of her head.

"I'm sure they just understood the signs that showed a change was coming," said Jessie. "So they didn't feel too worried about the Khan's request. In any case, if the day hadn't been sunny, they'd have come up with a reason. That's how these things work. Not that they don't believe in their own magic."

She sighed and added, "Right now I could use a bit of their faith."

Kat hesitated. Then she softly asked, "Jessie, are you afraid of the Khan?"

"I don't know, Kat," replied Jessie. "Maybe I am—a little. Though I think the astrologers worry me more. Perhaps I shouldn't have mentioned knowing about the stars. I didn't realize how important that knowledge was here. Or how much power it involves. I don't want to get in the middle of whatever's going on between Majeed and Sung."

They were interrupted by the thundering sound of horses galloping through the park. Curious, Kat and Jessie hurried outside. More than a dozen horsemen were charging through the snow, straight toward them. Leading the group was the Khan himself.

The horses slid to a stop, snorting and stamping. Kat and Jessie bowed before the Khan.

"Arise, ladies," said the Khan. "As you can see, I am off to the hunt."

That would explain the falcon perched on his shoulder, thought Kat.

"And it is you I have to thank, Lady Jessica," the Khan added.

Jessie stared at him in surprise. "What do you mean, your majesty?" she asked.

"Clearly it was your magic that changed the weather," said the Khan.

"But your astrologers—" Jessie began.

"The last time I ordered Majeed to improve the weather, he failed," the Khan said. "I am sure that he would have failed again without your help. You are very wise and powerful. I can sense it."

"Oh, but I'm sure I didn't—" Jessie started to protest.

Again the Khan interrupted. "No arguments," he said sharply. "I am never wrong about these things. Never."

"Of course not, your majesty," Jessie said quickly.

"You will join Sung and Majeed at the observatory today," said the Khan. "I have instructed them to listen to your words carefully. Teach them—and the others—everything you know."

Kat knew this wasn't good news. Not if there were already problems between Majeed and Sung.

However, as before, Jessie had no choice in the matter. She bowed once more. "I am honored, your majesty."

Without another word, the Khan whirled his horse about and rode off. His horsemen followed in a flurry of pounding hooves and waving manes.

As they headed back into their room, Kat turned to her aunt. "What did you do to make him think you changed the weather?" she asked.

"I told you," said Jessie. "I just chanted and sang along with the other astrologers. I had no idea that the Khan would give me the credit for the good weather."

"Well, now *I'm* worried," said Kat.

"I know," murmured Jessie. "Maybe we shouldn't stay. Maybe we should just go—"

She fell silent when a cold, unsmiling servant appeared in the doorway. It was plain that they wouldn't be deciding where to go—at least not for now. The Khan had already done that for them.

CHAPTER FOUR

A Snowy Ride

at paced the empty room, her thoughts racing. Should they return to their own time, as Jessie had suggested?

Kat didn't want to leave yet. But she'd rarely seen Jessie this concerned. If there was real danger, they couldn't stay.

A loud neigh came from the terrace. Kate opened the door to investigate. Perhaps the Khan had returned.

When she stepped outside, she saw two beautiful horses. But neither of them belonged to the Khan. On the back of a milky white mare sat Chin. She held the reins of the second animal—a small brown mare—in her hands.

"Oh!" Kat cried. Her excitement made her forget about her worries. "Is this your surprise?"

"Yes," laughed Chin. The white horse tossed its head and whinnied. "What do you think?"

"They're wonderful!" exclaimed Kat. "May I pet them?"

"Of course," responded Chin. With one swift motion, she slid off her horse and onto the ground.

Kat reached out and stroked Chin's horse gently on the muzzle. The other animal pushed its head forward for her touch.

"What are their names?" asked Kat.

"This is Desert Wind," replied Chin, placing her hand on

the brown horse. "And this is White Pearl," she added. "She comes from the Khan's special stock. He raises horses that are as white as the mountain snow."

"I would like you to meet my friend Kat," Chin said to White Pearl. At the same time, she gently tapped the animal's neck.

White Pearl tucked one front foot under her body and bowed to Kat.

"That's wonderful!" cried Kat. "How did she learn that trick?"

"I trained her myself," replied Chin with a proud smile. "She is the smartest horse I have ever worked with."

She fondly patted the white mare before turning back to Kat. "Now, would you like to ride Desert Wind?"

"Yes!" cried Kat. Then second thoughts hit her. Kat loved horses. She'd read every horse story in her library at least twice. However, she'd only been riding a few times. And while Chin's horses weren't that big, they seemed high-spirited.

She added, "I mean...I think I would. Desert Wind is trained too, isn't she?"

Chin nodded. "But perhaps you do not want to ride a horse. If you prefer, I could send for a camel or an elephant."

"Oh, no thank you," Kat replied. She had a sudden image of herself atop an elephant. "A horse will be fine."

"Then there is nothing to worry about," said Chin. "Desert Wind is gentle."

Chin steadied a stirrup, and Kat placed her foot in it. Taking a deep breath, she heaved herself up and into the saddle. The brown horse stood completely still.

Kat reached down and patted the mare's neck. Desert Wind's thick winter coat was soft and warm to the touch.

Chin remounted her own horse and started off across the palace grounds. Kat was glad to see that Desert Wind trailed along willingly.

They took a path that led around the lake. Although snow still lay thick in the shadows, spiky grass peeked through in the sunny spots. Kat began to relax and enjoy the rocking motion of her horse. Desert Wind was much easier to ride than the stable horses she had tried in the past.

Just as Kat was feeling confident, Chin and White Pearl took off at a gallop. Desert Wind wasted no time in following.

Chin and White Pearl moved as one, but Kat barely managed to stay in the saddle. She bounced wildly, slipping from side to side.

At last Chin pulled White Pearl to a halt. Desert Wind charged up alongside, then came to a quick stop as well. Kat cried out and gripped the horse's neck to keep from being thrown.

With a shaky gasp, she turned to Chin. The princess was staring at her in surprise. "Kat, are you all right?"

"I think so," replied Kat, pulling herself up to a sitting position. "I guess I don't know how to ride very well," she admitted.

"Forgive me for suggesting that we do this," said Chin. "I can return to the palace and have servants bring a sedan chair for you."

"Couldn't you just give me a lesson instead?" begged Kat. "I'd really love to learn. If you can get a horse to bow, surely you can teach me how to be a good rider."

Chin broke into a smile. "Of course I will teach you."

For the next few hours, they rode up and down the path. Chin showed Kat how to sit easily in the saddle. And she

taught Kat to use her knees and legs to control the horse. Before long Kat was riding smoothly—though not rapidly.

"Where did you learn to ride like you do?" asked Kat when they stopped to rest.

"In the deserts of Mongolia," said Chin. A sad look came over her face. "That is where I lived until I came to the Khan's court. The desert is truly wonderful, Kat. It is such a wild and beautiful place.

"White Pearl was born there as well," Chin continued. "I will take her to Persia with me. It will be like having a little piece of the desert with me always."

Kat couldn't help herself. "Chin, I think it's awful that you have to go to Persia. It's even worse that you've got to marry Argon."

"Awful?" asked Chin with surprise. "Why do you say that?"

"Well, you've never even met him," said Kat.

"What does that matter?" asked Chin. "There is no one else I wish to marry. And it is just as well that there is not. Majeed has read the signs. He has told the Khan that this marriage is good for the empire."

"For the empire, maybe," Kat repeated. "But what about for you?"

"Everyone speaks well of Argon. They say that my future husband is handsome and noble, although he is not young. Moreover, he is the Khan's own nephew—and ruler of all Persia!"

Kat sighed. "I hope you'll be happy with him."

"I will be happy doing the will of the Khan," declared Chin. "Besides, Majeed has told me many wonderful things about the Eight Kingdoms. He says that Persia is a place of wonder, with magicians who can do amazing things."

"But you said you'll miss Ta-tu," said Kat. "And the Mongolian desert."

"So I will," said Chin. "Yet I have always known that I might have to leave one day. I must do as the Khan commands me. And I am honored that he has chosen me as a wife for Argon."

Kat found all this more than a little hard to understand. Still, she had to admire Chin's courage. Here she was, getting ready to make a journey of thousands of miles. And to a place where she knew no one!

In a way, she'll be traveling even farther than Jessie and I have, thought Kat. At least we know that we can go home in the blink of an eye.

Chin started down the trail, Kat and Desert Wind at her side.

"Enough of my stories. Perhaps you could tell me about England," suggested Chin as they rode along. "Though I understand you may not remember much. It is such a long journey. You must have been very small when you left."

For several moments, Kat was silent. She wasn't sure what to say. She couldn't explain the real reason she knew so little about thirteenth-century England.

"I'll tell you what I can," Kat began. "For one thing, the country is ruled by a king, not an emperor." She went on to describe the huge stone castles and small thatched cottages of England. And there were things that Ta-tu and England had in common, she assured Chin. Like feasts and horses and snow.

A loud snort from White Pearl interrupted Kat. A lone rider was approaching at a gallop.

Chin shaded her eyes to see who was coming. "It is one

of the servants. He attends the astrologers," she announced. "I wonder why he is hurrying this way."

The rider pulled his horse to a stop in front of Chin. "I have a message for you, princess," he announced. "You are wanted in the palace. Sung has requested that you meet with him at once."

If Chin was surprised, she didn't show it. She simply nodded. "As he wishes."

At that, the servant turned his horse and trotted back to the palace.

"Sung," said Chin in a low voice. "This cannot be good news."

"Why are you upset about meeting with him?" Kat asked.

"I do not trust the man," answered Chin in a low voice. "He has only one interest. And that is increasing his own power in the Khan's court."

"But I thought he was friendlier than Majeed," said Kat. "At least he seems that way to me."

"Oh, you are right, Kat," said Chin. "Sung is happy about your coming here. After all, he had predicted that such a thing would come to pass. The Khan is most impressed that Sung was correct."

"I've been wondering about that," said Kat. "What exactly did he say would happen?"

"Just that important visitors would come from the West. Majeed disagreed and said the signs showed no such thing."

Chin sighed. "Majeed was wrong. But that is not the only reason why he is unfriendly to you. Majeed thinks the Khan should have nothing to do with visitors from Europe. He would even like to see the Polos leave. Yet they have been here for many years."

Chin urged her horse forward, and Kat followed.

"However, Majeed is a good man," the princess added. "He is loyal to the Khan and to the empire. I would trust him with my life."

Kat couldn't think of a suitable reply. So she and Chin rode in silence the rest of the way to the stables.

Inside the palace, they found Sung waiting. The Chinese astrologer rushed forward.

"Good day," he said, nodding to Kat. Then he turned his attention to Chin. "I bring you wonderful news, princess. I know how sad you have been about leaving China. And now it appears that you will not go to Persia after all."

"What do you mean?" asked Chin with surprise.

"There have been signs about your marriage," said Sung. "Signs that show that Argon is not the husband for you. Instead, you are to marry the governor of one of our northern provinces."

Chin had drawn back in shock at the news. Now she leaned forward once more, her face pale and tense. In a whisper, she asked, "Not Lord Tendu?"

Sung beamed. "None other, Princess Cocachin."

CHAPTER FIVE

A Spy in the Marketplace

Kat saw that Chin's face had grown still paler. Sung must have noticed the princess's reaction too. For he added with a purr, "The Khan seems to think it would be a good match. Better, indeed, than the marriage between you and Argon."

Chin turned away for a moment. When she looked at the astrologer again, her expression was blank. "I will be honored by whatever choice the Khan makes for me."

"Of course you will," said Sung.

"Is it certain that I shall marry Lord Tendu?" she asked in a flat voice.

"Almost certain," replied the astrologer. "The Khan has asked for time to consider the matter. Still, he agrees that all signs appear to point to such a marriage."

"Very well, then," said Chin quietly.

"Truly, it *is* very well," agreed Sung. With a swing of his robes, he marched off down the hall.

"Lord Tendu," whispered Chin when Sung was out of earshot. Her voice was filled with misery.

"What's wrong, Chin?" asked Kat. "What do you know about him?"

"I have heard that he is evil and cruel," said Chin. "There is not a princess in all the empire who wishes to marry him."

"Isn't there anything you can do?" asked Kat. "Maybe Sung was wrong about the signs. Though he certainly seems happy about this news."

"That is because Sung sees a way to build his power in the northern provinces," said Chin bitterly. "By promising a member of the Khan's court as a bride, he will win favor there. He has long wanted the Khan to consider this marriage. I foolishly believed that it would never happen."

"Maybe the other astrologers will say something different," suggested Kat.

"I am afraid that is too much to hope for," murmured Chin. "Especially now that Sung is in such favor with the Khan."

Chin shook her head. "What is to happen, will happen. But now I must let you return to your quarters to rest after our long ride. I will call a servant to guide you there."

Kat was quiet as she trailed after the servant. It's bad enough that Chin has to marry someone she's never met, she thought. Now on top of that, it's someone cruel.

Another thing troubled Kat. Sung had said that visitors from the West would arrive. By turning up in Ta-tu, she and Jessie had proved him right. As a result, the Khan was more willing to listen to Sung now. So in a horrible way, the change in Chin's marriage plans were their fault.

~

A soak in the bath, a walk in the park, a stroll through the palace. None of that did anything to take Kat's mind off Chin's problem.

Finally, at the end of the long afternoon, Jessie returned to the room. Kat wasted no time in telling her aunt what had happened. She also explained why she thought they were responsible.

At the end of Kat's story, Jessie sighed. "I don't know what we should do. I'm sure the astrologers won't listen to me. Chin's absolutely right about Majeed not wanting us here. He doesn't even pretend to like the fact that I'm allowed into the observatory."

"What about Sung?" asked Kat. "He has a reason to be friendly toward you."

"To be honest, he worries me even more," replied Jessie. "Today he asked me question after question. He seems to be trying to show everyone that he's far wiser than I am."

"Why would he act that way?" asked Kat. "Chin says Sung has greater influence with the Khan because we showed up. He should be happy to have you around."

"It seems the Khan told the astrologers that my 'powers' are greater than theirs. Needless to say, that hasn't made me very popular. I'm afraid we may have ended up in the middle of something dangerous."

Kat knew what was coming next. Sure enough, Jessie said, "I think we should go home."

"We can't, Jessie. Not if Chin is in this mess because of us!"

Jessie hesitated before answering. "I agree that her problem may be at least partly our fault," she admitted. "But I'm worried that staying might make it even worse for Chin. And for ourselves."

"We can't just take off!" exclaimed Kat. "Not without trying to set things right."

"I understand, Kat," said Jessie. "Let's both think about this for a while. Tomorrow we can talk about our choices. Maybe there's a way I can fix things between Majeed and

Sung. And a way to solve Chin's problem. Meanwhile, we both have to be careful."

The arrival of a serving girl ended the conversation. She brought news from the Khan.

"Because of the good weather, there will be an outdoor market tomorrow," the girl said. "The Khan has arranged for you to attend with a group from his court." She bowed and left the room.

Kat noticed a gleam of interest in her aunt's eyes. "It's a good thing we'll still be here tomorrow, isn't it?" Kat said with a grin.

Jessie laughed. "I admit it—I wouldn't want to miss this opportunity. But remember, once we've seen the marketplace, we have to have a serious talk. Then we'll decide how long we're staying."

<hr>

Kat and Jessie woke to another pleasant winter day. They dressed quickly, putting on warm clothing for their outing.

Kat fished a handful of paper out of her woolen bag. "This has to be money," she said. "I checked in the encyclopedia, and it said Kublai Khan used paper money. Besides, I put some coins into my bag before we left. I'm sure this is what they changed into."

She handed a few bills to Jessie. Then she dug into the bag again. This time she pulled out the instant camera. "I haven't used this yet," she said thoughtfully. She dropped it back into her bag.

"Be careful," Jessie warned. "You can't let anyone see it."

"I know," Kat said. "I'll keep it out of sight. I'd just like to get a picture of the marketplace."

Before long they heard a knock at the outside doors. They opened them to discover two sedan chairs. Each was carried by a pair of servants. The men set the chairs down on the ground, and Kat and Jessie climbed inside. Then the chairs were lifted into the air.

Kat felt strange about being carried around in such a manner. But she knew that these men earned their living by doing just that. So she sat back to enjoy the ride.

They soon joined up with many others. Kat knew that Chin wouldn't be coming. The princess had much to do to prepare for her marriage. But she was pleased to see Marco, who nodded a greeting.

Kat noted that Majeed and Sung were also part of the group. I'm going to stay away from them, she decided.

Soon they set off for the market. In single file, the sedan chairs were carried across the palace grounds and into the city.

They stopped at the edge of a crowded square. Colorful stalls had been set up, and tables of goods were everywhere. Everything imaginable was being sold—from cloth to drums to furniture. Rich smells and strange sounds filled the air.

The servants set down the chairs, and Marco joined Kat and Jessie.

"This is fantastic!" exclaimed Kat.

"Indeed," said Marco. "The markets of Ta-tu are filled with wonders from all over. I would be happy to tell you about them."

"We'd love to have you as our guide," said Jessie. "There are so many beautiful things here!"

"Many of the merchants offer especially fine goods now,"

explained Marco. "They know people are searching for things to give the Khan."

When Kat seemed puzzled, Marco explained. "New Year gifts. The holiday is very near. It is the custom to offer gifts to the Khan."

"Then we should buy something too," said Jessie. "What kinds of things does he receive?"

"Gifts of gold and silver," replied Marco. "White is also an important New Year color. And since the Khan considers nine a lucky number, he is often given that many gifts. Or if the giver is very rich, nine times nine."

"Nine times nine?" asked Kat.

"Yes," said Marco. "I have seen this with my own eyes. The Khan might receive 81 fine horses. Or 81 bowls made of gold or silver."

Jessie and Kat exchanged glances. They hadn't realized just how important this occasion was. Could they find a gift that would mean anything to the Khan? And if they did, could they afford to buy it?

With Marco, they began to make their way through the marketplace. As they explored the square, they found that it was more than just a place for selling goods. Street musicians wandered by playing spirited tunes. Brightly dressed men and women threw sticks and dice to tell fortunes.

Marco was a wonderful guide. He had actually traveled to many of the places from which the market goods had come. Near a weaver's stall, he told of watching women make cloth from threads of solid gold. And at a fruit stand, he described melons he had once eaten. "The taste of sunshine," he said.

When Kat exclaimed at the unusual animals for sale, Marco laughed.

"Ah, Katherine," he said. "If you had but seen some of the strange creatures I have encountered. Why, I once saw a snake with legs—and enormous eyes atop its head. It was ten paces long and as thick around as a man. Besides being huge, it had a long mouth filled with teeth as sharp as knives. Truly a beast more fearsome than any you see here."

For a moment, Kat thought that Marco might be making the animal up. Then she realized that he must be talking about a crocodile!

As they made their way around the square, Kat wished she could take a picture. But the marketplace was so crowded that she didn't dare. The camera stayed hidden away in her woolen bag.

By mid-afternoon, they had grown hungry. So the three stopped at a food stall. After buying dishes of spicy rice, they settled on a nearby bench.

When they finished eating, Marco explained that he had to do something for the Khan. "I will find you before it is time for us to leave," he promised.

Kat and Jessie continued to wander the marketplace by themselves. They passed merchants selling bright jewelry, bowls of gold and silver, and fine pottery. At each stall, they searched for something to give the Khan.

"Of course, we'll probably be gone before the New Year feast," warned Jessie.

"We don't know that for sure," argued Kat. "We'd better have something, just in case."

At last they reached a stall filled from top to bottom with

silk hangings. Some even had gemstones or pearls woven into the design.

Kat was drawn to one hanging. It was made of silk so white that it seemed to sparkle. Gold and silver threads fringed the edges.

"Maybe we could give this to the Khan," she suggested. "It's not the same as giving 81 horses, but it *is* beautiful."

"I think that's a good idea," Jessie agreed. "At least it has all the right colors—white, silver, and gold."

They bargained with the merchant and finally settled on an amount. Earlier they'd asked Marco to explain the money, so they knew which bills to use.

With their purchase wrapped up, Kat and Jessie moved on. They found themselves just as interested in watching the people as in looking at the goods.

Then, near the opening of a curtained stall, something caught Kat's eye. It looked like a large plate covered with drawings. Beside it hung a smooth wooden stick.

A gong, Kat realized. The stick would be used to ring it. She was about to pass by, but the markings on the gong stopped her in her tracks. At once Kat moved into the stall for a closer look, pulling Jessie along with her.

"What is it?" her aunt asked.

Kat traced the markings with her finger. A circle of symbols surrounded an image of the sun. And the symbols seemed strangely familiar.

"Jessie," she whispered. "Don't these look a lot like...?"

"The drawings on our medallions!" finished Jessie.

The shopkeeper, hoping to sell something, drew closer.

"Sir, can you tell us what these markings mean?" Kat asked.

"They are ancient magical signs," explained the merchant. "It is said that they bring great power."

"But what do they mean?" asked Jessie.

"No one knows for sure," said the man. "Still, one does not need to understand the magic in order for it to work."

He looked at them expectantly, but Jessie politely explained, "I'm sorry, we're travelers. We couldn't take the gong with us. We were just admiring its beauty."

With a shrug, the merchant turned to another customer.

As soon as he was busy, Kat pulled her medallion out from under her clothing. She held it up and compared it to the gong.

"Not exactly the same," she murmured. "But close. Do you think this means anything, Jessie?"

Jessie shook her head. "I wish I knew. There's no way to tell where and when Malcolm got the medallions."

Kat tucked her medallion back into hiding. "Still, it's funny that the symbols on the gong mean great power. And the medallions are our power source. I wonder—"

She broke off with a gasp as her eyes traveled to a slit in the back curtain of the stall. Peering through the opening was a single human eye!

CHAPTER SIX

The Polos' Problem

ho's there?" Kat cried.

At once the eye disappeared.

Kat dashed outside and around the corner. But there was no one behind the stall.

She gazed around the marketplace. All she had seen was one gleaming black eye. There was no way to pick out the watcher from the crowd.

Jessie joined her outside. "What's going on?" she asked.

Kat explained in a low, worried voice. At the end, she added, "Why would someone be spying on us? Do you think he saw my medallion?"

"Even if he—or she—did, I wouldn't worry about it," Jessie said. "Almost everyone here wears beautiful jewelry of some sort. I can't believe anyone would be interested in our simple medallions. Your 'spy' was probably just curious to see two ladies from the West."

"I suppose you're right," admitted Kat.

They moved back into the bustle of the marketplace. Kat tried to shake off her concern. But an uneasy feeling remained with her.

By now the early darkness of winter was settling over the square. The air grew colder. Lanterns began to flicker in stalls. Still, the marketplace was as busy as it had been by day.

Then something whistled and shot into the sky. There was a burst of sparks high above the crowd.

"Fireworks!" cried Kat. She stared in wonder at the trails of colored light.

Jessie smiled. "I'd forgotten that the Chinese were the first to know how to do this."

They watched in fascination as one bright explosion followed another. In all the noise, they didn't hear Marco approach.

"Katherine and Lady Jessica! I have been looking for you."

They spun around to greet him.

"I am sorry I was gone for so long," Marco said. "And now I am afraid it is time to leave."

As they walked toward the sedan chairs, Marco asked if they had found a gift.

"Yes," replied Kat. "Though certainly nothing as wonderful as 81 horses!"

"Do not worry about that," laughed Marco. "The Khan is delighted to have you here in Ta-tu. Learning about other people and places gives him great pleasure. That is one reason I admire the emperor. For I am much the same way."

"So am I," said Kat with a smile.

~~

True to her word, Jessie had done a lot of thinking about whether they should leave. And by the next morning, she'd come up with a plan.

"I don't think I can do anything to convince Majeed that having me here is good," she admitted. "But at least I can relieve Sung's worries about how powerful I am. That may improve things between the two astrologers."

"What are you going to do?" asked Kat.

"I'll ask him all kinds of questions. Before long he'll be sure I don't know enough to be any danger to him. And I'll keep telling the Khan how wonderful his astrologers are. Once we have that taken care of, we'll decide what to do about Chin—if anything."

Kat was relieved that Jessie had agreed to stay. So she decided not to mention her worries about the watcher at the marketplace again. She told herself that she'd made too much out of the matter.

As Kat and Jessie finished dressing, a servant came in with their breakfast. Kat noted that it wasn't the usual friendly girl. Instead, an older woman carried their tray. Kat recognized her. The stiff back and stern face would be hard to forget. But at first she couldn't remember where they'd run into each other.

Then it came to her. This was the woman who had led Jessie to the astrologers.

"I am Li. I will be serving you from now on," announced the woman in a cold voice.

"What happened to the other girl?" Kat asked.

A hint of a frown crossed the woman's forehead. "She has been sent back to her home. She was far too slow and careless to serve such honored guests."

Kat and Jessie were puzzled. They had certainly never complained. In fact, they had enjoyed the girl's cheerful chatter.

Clearly there would be no such chatter from Li. In a businesslike manner, she set out the food. She stood back and bowed. "I will wait outside until you are done, Lady Jessica. Then I am to take you to the observatory."

Jessie hurried through breakfast and went to join Li. Left to herself, Kat toyed with some ideas for how to spend the day. Chin was busy preparing for the New Year and wouldn't be free until later.

Then Kat brightened. She could use this time to do something she'd been wanting to do. She could take pictures of the palace gardens. Quickly she put on her heavy fur coat and headed outside.

Once again Kat marveled at the sights. Even in the winter, the gardens were beautiful. Stone bridges and fountains stood at every turn, while graceful trees towered overhead. Chin had explained that many of these trees were rare and had come from faraway places. They had been dug up fully grown and carried to Ta-tu by elephants!

Kat checked to be sure that no one was in sight. Then she snapped a photo of an interesting fountain. The camera whirred and spit out a square of heavy paper. Kat watched the image take form before tucking the picture away.

She was about to take another snapshot when a loud voice made her jump.

"No! I refuse to consider such a thing!"

It was the Khan, Kat realized. And he sounded angry. She heard other voices as well. In comparison, however, they were soft and respectful.

Kat moved closer as the Khan continued.

"We have spoken of this matter before, my friends. My wishes have not changed since then."

By now Kat couldn't control her curiosity. She wanted to hear the other side of this conversation. And, if possible, to take a photo of the Khan. Her footsteps silenced by her soft boots, she made her way along the great walls.

Kat rounded a corner and stopped in the shadow of the wall. Before her stretched the parade grounds that fronted the palace. The Khan was there, on horseback. At some distance behind him waited a group of fellow hunters. And in front of the emperor stood Marco, his father, and his uncle.

No one was looking her way, so Kat took several pictures. Then she hid the camera again and listened.

"Your majesty—" Marco began.

"Enough, Marco!" declared the Khan. "I will hear no more of this."

With that, the Khan wheeled his horse around and charged off. The rest of the hunting party followed. Soon the only ones left in sight were the Polos, who spoke to one another in whispers.

Kat hesitated for a moment. Should she try to find out what was wrong? But she decided not to. The Polos might be uncomfortable knowing that she'd overheard the argument.

So Kat continued on her stroll through the gardens. She set off toward a wooden pavilion that stood atop a hill. It would make a perfect picture.

She was just reaching for the camera when she heard a sound behind her. It was Marco, and he was headed her way. Kat let the camera drop back into her bag.

Kat quickly realized that Marco hadn't even seen her. His

eyes were on the path; his mind seemed to be miles away.

"Hello," called Kat in a soft voice.

Marco started and looked around. When his eyes fell on Kat, he asked quietly, "How are you, Katherine?"

"I'm fine," answered Kat. "But you seem upset. Is something wrong?"

Marco sighed. "It is a long story," he said. Then he laughed bitterly. "Which is really the problem. It is a *very* long story. And I had hoped it was coming to an end."

He saw Kat's puzzled expression and motioned to a stone bench. "Sit down. I feel the need to talk—if you are willing to listen."

"Of course," replied Kat, taking a seat. Marco settled beside her. For a moment, he gazed out at the gardens.

"As you know, my father and uncle and I have been here for 17 years," he began. "So I have served the Khan for half my life."

"That's a long time to be away from home," observed Kat.

"Much too long," sighed Marco. "We have asked the Khan for permission to leave more than once. Now he commands us not to ask again."

"What?" exclaimed Kat. "Can he do that?"

"Oh yes," replied Marco. "He is the ruler of this land—and of those within its borders."

Marco noted the shocked look on Kat's face. "Do not misunderstand," he said. "The Khan has been very good to us. We respect him and do not wish to offend him."

"But he must see why you want to go home," said Kat. "At least for a while. What if you promise to come back?"

"The Khan is old. He knows he does not have much longer to live. You came all the way from England, Katherine.

So you realize that the trip takes many years. Even if we did return, it would be too late for the Khan."

"It still doesn't seem right that you should be forced to stay."

"It is not a matter of right or wrong," Marco explained. "It is a matter of what is. We will be here for the lifetime of the Khan, I fear."

"Maybe you should talk to Majeed," said Kat. "The Khan listens to his astrologers. And from what I've heard, Majeed would suggest that you leave."

Marco gave a short, harsh laugh. "He would. In fact, he has done so before. But the Khan did not listen then. And he surely will not listen now. Not with Sung in greater favor than Majeed. No, there are no easy answers to our problem."

With a shake of his head, Marco rose. "I have worried you long enough with my troubles. Thank you for listening."

After Marco had left, Kat stayed on the bench, thinking. There had to be some way to convince the Khan to let the Polos leave.

At last Kat's teeth began to chatter. Time to head back to the palace, she decided. It was warm enough for walking in the gardens. But it was too cold to sit for more than a few minutes. Besides, there was something she had to find out.

Back in her room, Kat fished the encyclopedia out of Jessie's bag. "I know the Polos returned to Europe," she whispered. "I wonder if I can find out when."

Kat flipped to the section that told about Marco and his travels. Her eyes lit on one sentence.

"I knew it," she said softly. "Something is wrong—very wrong!"

The Flame of Truth

What do you mean? What's wrong?"

Book in hand, Kat spun around. "Jessie! I'm glad you're back!" Quickly she repeated her conversation with Marco.

"But the Khan *has* to let the Polos go," Kat continued. "The encyclopedia says Marco was in China for 17 years. That means he's supposed to leave right about now."

Jessie read the section Kat pointed out. "That's what it says," she agreed. "Maybe the Polos will leave later this year."

"And maybe they won't!" cried Kat. "By coming here, we might have changed things for them as well as for Chin. This could be our fault too!"

"Kat, you don't know—" began Jessie.

"I *do* know that we seem to have upset things!" interrupted Kat.

"I can't argue with that," Jessie admitted. "However, it's not really *we*. It's *me.*"

She went on, "Still, things went better today, Kat. Sung, at least, acted like he was less worried about having me here."

"I'm beginning to think that might be a mistake," said Kat as a plan formed in her mind. "Maybe we want the astrologers to believe your powers are greater than theirs after all."

"What do you mean?" asked Jessie suspiciously.

Kat took a deep breath and described her plan. As she finished, she added, "So if this works, we'll have solved Chin's problem—and the Polos' too."

Jessie was silent for a time. Finally she said, "All right, I'm willing to try it. As long as we make one change to the plan."

"Great!" exclaimed Kat. "What do you want to change?"

"I won't be the one showing off my powers. You will."

"But—" began Kat.

"Think about it, Kat," Jessie broke in. "It will be even more impressive if you—a mere child—perform this magic. And the astrologers won't be as quick to suspect you."

The thought made Kat nervous. Still, she could understand Jessie's reasoning. "I'll do it," she agreed. "But we'll need some help from Chin. She's meeting me here this afternoon."

"Okay," said Jessie. "Remember, though, we can't tell her everything."

By the time Chin appeared, Kat and Jessie had agreed on just what to say.

"Good afternoon, Lady Jessica," said Chin with a smile. She looked at Kat. "Do you want to go riding?" she asked.

"Can we do something else instead?" asked Kat.

"Of course," replied Chin. "Just tell me what you wish to do, and I will try to make it possible."

As Kat explained, Chin's expression went from confusion to hope. "I do not fully understand," she said at last. "But I will gladly help. What do you need from me?"

~

Soon everything was ready. Chin had helped them set things up. Jessie sent word to the astrologers, who sent word to the Khan. And the emperor ended up summoning Kat and

Jessie. After Kat changed into a sweeping robe that she thought suited her role, they set off.

At the entrance to the great hall, Jessie turned to Kat. "Ready?" she whispered. Kat nodded, too excited to speak.

Inside the hall, the Khan was waiting. As usual, Majeed and Sung stood close by. The Polos were there as well. Kat also noticed dozens of other astrologers, members of the court, and Chin.

"My astrologers tell me you bring an important message," said the Khan to Jessie.

Both Majeed and Sung shot Jessie questioning looks. Clearly they wondered about her purpose in asking for this meeting.

"That is true, your majesty," Jessie replied calmly. "But I am not the one who brings this message. It is my niece."

Shocked whispers passed through the onlookers.

"Your niece?" asked the Khan in surprise. "This child?"

"Yes," said Jessie. "Katherine has great gifts, you see. Oh, she's not as skilled as your astrologers," she quickly added. "Still, I would ask you to listen to her."

"Very well," said the Khan. "Katherine, let us hear this message."

Trembling a little, Katherine handed over the sheet of paper she'd been carrying. "It is here, your majesty."

The Khan studied it closely. "I can see nothing!" he protested.

"Perhaps you cannot see the words," said Kat boldly. "But to my eyes, they are clear. And I believe that they are about Princess Cocachin's marriage."

At that, Sung leaned forward to look at the paper. "Nonsense!" he snarled. In a softer voice, he addressed the

Khan. "Your majesty, anyone can read what they wish from blank paper. The girl's words mean nothing. She has no magic."

The Khan frowned and handed the paper back to Kat. "Explain yourself, Katherine."

With a serious look, Kat declared, "I will make the words clear to you, your majesty. If you wish me to."

"I command you to do so," replied the Khan.

"I must have a lighted lantern," Kat said. "And the help of your chief astrologers."

At a nod from the Khan, Sung and Majeed stepped closer. Then at Kat's request, Sung held a lantern in front of him.

"Behold!" Kat cried. "The Flame of Truth!"

She carefully held the paper over the lantern. The paper needed to be close to the heat, but not close enough to catch fire.

As Kat moved the sheet back and forth, brown images began to form. Gradually they became clear symbols in Mongolian writing.

Sung was the first to react. His eyes widened in astonishment. Startled cries ran through the crowd as other onlookers noticed. Even to Kat, it seemed as though the words appeared by magic.

"What does it say?" demanded the Khan, who was too far away to see the symbols clearly.

In a shaky voice, Majeed read the words aloud: "Eight Kingdoms."

"Eight Kingdoms!" repeated the Khan. "Does this mean what I think it does?"

"I believe it means that Chin must go to the Eight Kingdoms of Persia, your majesty," said Kat softly. "But you

should ask your astrologers if they agree." She held her breath. What if things didn't go as she and Jessie hoped?

Sung put down the lantern. Then both astrologers bent over the paper, studying the symbols. They spoke too quietly to be heard. Still, it was plain that they were arguing.

Finally the two men turned to face the Khan. Majeed looked pleased, while Sung wore a fierce frown.

It was Sung who addressed the Khan. "I—er—we are able to read this sign clearly, your majesty," he announced crossly. "Princess Cocachin must go to Persia. She must marry Argon, the ruler of the Eight Kingdoms."

"Is this your understanding as well, Majeed?" asked the Khan.

The other astrologer nodded. "It is."

Kat held back a smile. The trick had worked. She had asked Chin how to write the words she needed. But she had used goat's milk in place of ink. The milk was invisible until heat turned it brown. And once the words appeared, their meaning was clear to everyone. Even Sung hadn't dared see anything different in them.

However, Kat wasn't finished yet. "There is more to my message, your majesty," she said. "The princess cannot travel to Persia alone. She must be taken there by wise, experienced travelers."

The Khan stared at Kat. At last he nodded his head in agreement. And just as Kat had expected, he raised his hand to summon the Polos. After all, who was better suited for this task?

At that moment, Sung whispered something to the Khan. What's he up to? wondered Kat.

"Of course I do not wish them to leave," murmured the

Khan to his astrologer. "Yet what choice do I have?"

Sung whispered again. "Ah yes, I see," replied the Khan. "Your advice is most wise, Sung."

The emperor turned back to the crowd. "I have made my decision," he stated. "Princess Cocachin shall have the best of guides. She shall go to Persia in the company of Lady Jessica and Katherine."

CHAPTER EIGHT

Meddling with Magic

What have I done? thought Kat.

Yes, she'd managed to solve Chin's problem. But the Polos were still trapped in China. And she and Jessie were to set out on a trip that would take years!

Jessie spoke first. She suggested calmly, "Great Khan, you must choose someone else. We are unworthy of this honor."

"Unworthy!" growled the Khan. "Nonsense! If I say you are worthy, then you are worthy."

In a silky voice, Sung added, "You are wise, your majesty—as always. The signs point to the English magicians."

Kat was sure she knew what was going through Sung's mind. Now he thought he had reason to fear both Kat and Jessie. He wanted them out of China as much as Majeed did.

Quietly she asked, "Are you sure that is what the signs say? Or only what *you* say?"

Sung's eyes snapped with anger. But it was the Khan who asked for an explanation. "What do you mean, child?"

"Forgive me, your majesty," said Kat. "It is only that the sign I showed you was not clear about this matter."

Kat could sense Jessie's discomfort. Though it was risky, Kat had to make the Khan question his own decision.

"Explain yourself," the emperor commanded.

"The sign clearly showed that the marriage to Argon

should take place," said Kat. "But it was not clear about who is meant to guide the princess safely to Persia.

"My aunt and I would be honored to do so," she added. "However, I would like to seek another sign. One that shows who should have this important task."

"Hmmm," said the Khan thoughtfully. "It is true that you did not see who should be her guide."

A tense silence fell over the hall. All eyes were on the Khan, waiting for his decision.

Kat held her breath. If the Khan asked his astrologers to search for a further sign, her hopes were dead. But if he'd been impressed by Kat's "magic," he might turn to her instead.

"What would you suggest, Katherine?" the Khan asked.

"I would like to think about the matter, Great Khan," said Kat. "Then I will come before you again with a clearer sign."

"So be it!" announced the Khan. "Return here at dusk."

Kat bowed. With Jessie at her side, she headed out of the hall. They passed the Polos, who looked as if their last hope might soon be taken from them. They also passed Chin, whose eyes shone with thanks.

Back in their room, Jessie demanded, "Kat! What were you thinking? What's all this about another sign?"

"I have an idea," replied Kat.

Slowly she explained. And slowly the frown on Jessie's face melted.

~

It was almost time to return to the reception hall. Kat and Jessie were going over their plan one last time.

"Just don't forget your part," said Kat. "You have to get the Polos to stand close together." It was at least the fifth time she'd reminded Jessie of that fact.

"I'll do my best." Jessie shook her head and laughed. "This idea is just crazy enough that it might work. Still, if it doesn't, don't forget what I said. At the first sign of trouble, I'm stepping in. I'll get us back to the room somehow, and we'll go home immediately."

She stood up and took a deep breath. "It's time to leave."

Kat checked the folds of her robe. The long, bell-shaped sleeves hid her hands completely. "I'm ready," she announced.

They hurried to the hall, each lost in her own thoughts.

When Kat and Jessie stepped through the door, a hush fell over the crowd. Thank goodness, thought Kat as she made her way toward the Khan. The Polos are just about where I want them to be. Marco stood by himself, his eyes downcast. His uncle and father were speaking together not far from his side.

Kat and Jessie stopped in front of the Khan. Jessie bowed, then moved back near the Polos. Kat saw her aunt whisper to Marco, who responded with a puzzled look. But Kat noticed that he stepped slightly closer to his uncle and father.

Kat bowed low. Her clasped hands were hidden by the sleeves of her robe. "Thank you for the gift of time, your majesty," she said. "I am ready to seek another sign."

Sung snorted, and Majeed stared at her coldly. But the Khan's face was open and filled with curiosity.

"Prepare yourselves!" Kat announced in a loud voice. "For this sign will come like a lightning bolt!"

She raised her clasped hands chest high and began to spin slowly in place. She made one complete turn, then another.

On her third turn, Kat paused briefly in front of the Polos. A flash of light seemed to burst from her fingertips.

The whirring sound that followed was lost in the cries

from the crowd. Even the Khan was alarmed. He rose halfway from his seat before sinking down again.

With all eyes fixed on her, Kat carefully pulled one hand out from her sleeve. In it she grasped a small square of paper. A border of white surrounded a center of smoky gray.

"Observe the sign!" she said as she placed the square on a table near the Khan.

The Khan drew back. But when there were no further bursts of light, he leaned over to study the paper.

"It is a trick!" cried Sung. "Another blank paper."

A gasp from the Khan stopped him. "Wait! I see something! It is a sign!"

Kat held her breath—as did almost everyone else in the room. Sung, Majeed, and others in the crowd edged closer to see the magical paper.

A blurry gray blotch began to form. Then the edges of the shape grew sharp, and bright colors appeared.

The Khan gazed at the photo, wonder in his eyes. "It is the Polos!" he cried. "Their image has appeared magically!"

The emperor's eyes went from the photo to the Polos themselves. "This is wondrous," he marveled. "More real than any painting I have ever seen. It is as if they themselves have been captured on this paper."

The Polos pushed forward to see this marvel. Marco shook his head in amazement.

Kat stepped back. "You have seen the sign," she said. "Now, Great Khan, it is time to turn to your astrologers. Let them explain its meaning."

Sung lifted his eyes to Kat's. He looked stunned. "The meaning is clear, your majesty," the astrologer said. "The Polos should escort the princess to Persia."

Majeed nodded his agreement.

"Then it shall be done," declared the Khan. His eyes went once again to the photograph.

"I must take this sign with me, your majesty," said Kat, trying not to sound nervous.

"I understand," the Khan replied sadly.

Kat reached forward to pluck the photo from the table. From the corner of one eye, she saw Sung slip away.

He's not very happy about this, Kat thought with satisfaction.

The photo safely in hand, Kat bowed. "Thank you, your majesty." Then she and Jessie moved toward the door.

When they were well outside the great room, Jessie allowed herself a grin. "You did it, Kat!" she whispered.

Before Kat could reply, they heard quick footsteps behind them. Chin rounded the corner, her face alight with joy.

"Kat! Lady Jessica! Wait!" she cried, hurrying to their side. "I do not understand your magic," she said softly. "But I do understand that you have done something wonderful for me. Thank you."

"The princess is not the only one who is grateful," added another voice. It was Marco, just coming around the corner himself.

"I must go," said Chin. "I will leave you with Marco." She smiled again and rushed back to the reception hall.

"The two of you are remarkable magicians," Marco declared. "We clearly owe you many, many thanks."

"You're very welcome," said Kat.

Marco hesitated. "I wonder...do you know anything about my future?"

Kat and Jessie exchanged a look. Then Jessie smiled and

answered. "We don't know everything that lies ahead for you, Marco. But we do know this: You will return to your home. And you must remember as much as you can about your travels. Someday you will share your story with the world.

"But we must ask one favor," Jessie added. "Please don't tell about what Kat did today. In fact, don't say anything about us at all."

"As you wish," Marco agreed. "However, I may regret this promise. Your magic deserves mention in any story I might tell."

He repeated his thanks and started back for the hall.

Kat and Jessie returned to their room. There Kat could at last remove the camera, which she'd clutched beneath the sleeve of her robe. Then the two great magicians sank onto their beds, more than ready to rest.

～

When Kat woke early the next day, Jessie was still asleep. Quietly Kat got up to dress.

For a minute, she studied the room. Where was the gown she'd worn yesterday morning? She thought back to when she'd changed into her magician's robe. She was sure she'd left the dress on a stool at the foot of her bed. Her medallion was with the gown too, tucked in the sleeve. She'd taken it off because it would have shown at the neck of the robe.

However, neither the dress—nor the medallion—was on the stool. And now that she thought about it, she hadn't seen them last night either.

"Maybe a servant put the dress back into the trunk," she whispered to herself.

Quickly she went to the wooden chest and picked through the clothing. To her relief, she soon found the gown, neatly folded away.

Kat pulled out the gown and fumbled in the sleeve. No medallion. "I must have put it in the other sleeve," she told herself. Yet the medallion wasn't there either.

Wildly Kat began pulling things out of the trunk. She felt in pockets and sleeves. She ran her hands across the bottom of the trunk.

But it was no use. The medallion was gone!

A Terrible Loss

essie! Wake up!" Kat called. She hurried over to the bed where her aunt lay sleeping.

"What is it?" mumbled Jessie.

"My medallion!" Kat cried. "It's gone!"

At that, Jessie was wide awake. "What?" she exclaimed as she sat up. "It can't be! Weren't you wearing it?"

Kat explained why she'd removed the medallion and where she'd hidden it.

"Okay, let's not panic," said Jessie. "It must be here somewhere. We'll just have to search. But first I'd better see if mine is safe. And whether the time machine is still in the trunk."

"The machine is there," sighed Kat. "I opened the bag and checked while I was looking through the chest."

"And the silver medallion is right where I put it last night," said Jessie. She reached into the toe of her slipper and pulled out her medallion. "Now let's see if we can find yours."

For the next several minutes, Kat joined her aunt in searching the room. They checked everywhere. However, they didn't turn up the gold medallion.

Finally Kat looked over at her aunt. "Jessie, I'm afraid someone stole it!"

"Stole it?" echoed Jessie. "How? And why? As a piece of jewelry, it's worthless compared to what everyone else here wears."

"The 'how' would have been easy," replied Kat. "There are servants in and out of our room all day long. And as for why..." She trailed off.

When Kat spoke again, she sounded even more worried. "I can't help thinking that this ties in to what happened at the market. What if whoever was watching from outside the tent heard us? The merchant told us that the markings on the gong meant power. And I said that the markings on my medallion looked the same. Maybe the thief believes the medallion has magical powers!"

Jessie sighed. "In a way, the thief would be right. Without both medallions, we can't start up the time machine. We're stuck here in the past."

"I know. And it's my fault too. I should have given the medallion to you for safekeeping. I was so busy thinking about my plans that I got careless. Now what can we do?"

Jessie nervously ran her fingers through her hair. "All right, who'd be most likely to want the 'power' of the medallion?"

"The astrologers!" Kat cried. "They're the ones who've been worrying about your powers."

"And yours too, after yesterday's little magic show," Jessie reminded her.

A sudden thought struck Kat. "Li!" she exclaimed. "The new servant. We know she works for the astrologers, Jessie. I bet they sent away the other serving girl. That way Li would have a reason to be in our room."

Kat continued. "I noticed that Sung left the hall before we did yesterday. He probably went to get Li. And she could have stolen the medallion before we returned to the room."

"You're probably right," agreed Jessie. "But we can't just

walk up to her and ask for it back. We'll need some proof."

"I'll see what I can find out," said Kat. "And you're supposed to go to the observatory again today. So you'll have a chance to do a little detective work too."

"I'll try," said Jessie. "But, Kat, promise me you'll be careful about whom you question."

"I promise."

A knock at the door ended their discussion.

"Come in," called Jessie.

A servant entered with their breakfast. But it wasn't Li. Once again it was a stranger.

As the serving girl set out their meal, Kat questioned her. She learned that Li had left the palace. None of the servants knew where she had gone—or why.

After the girl left, Kat turned to her aunt. "Li has to be the thief! And now the astrologers have sent her away so we can't talk to her!"

"Don't jump to conclusions, Kat," warned Jessie. "Let's see what we learn today."

Soon Jessie was on her way to the observatory. And Kat headed to the stables. Chin had promised to give her another riding lesson. Kat wasn't sure she felt like riding, but she did want to talk to Chin.

Kat found the princess brushing White Pearl's soft coat.

Chin looked up with a warm smile. "Good morning, Kat. I am pleased to see you. I want to thank you again. I am sure that I will be happy in Persia."

"I'm glad I could help," said Kat. Then, before Kat could get to her own questions, Chin made an announcement.

"I want to show you something," she said.

Chin tied a line to White Pearl's halter and led the mare

70

off a little way. Then she shook the line and lifted one hand in the air.

White Pearl reared up on her hind legs. For a few moments, the mare stood there, perfectly balanced. Then she came back down on all fours.

As Chin walked away from her, White Pearl followed. With her first step, the mare lifted one front foot high off the ground. She held it there for several seconds before taking the next step. The beautiful horse was dancing!

After a dozen steps, Chin turned and bowed to Kat. White Pearl bowed too.

"That's fantastic!" said Kat. "How did you ever teach her all that?"

"It took many hours of practice," Chin admitted. "But White Pearl can learn anything." She hugged the horse, then added, "White Pearl will dance for the emperor when I present his gift."

"That's a wonderful idea!" agreed Kat. Curious, she asked, "What are you giving the Khan?"

"A saddle blanket," replied Chin. "I have been working on it for weeks. Though I would like to give him something more special. Particularly since this will be my last time to celebrate the New Year at Ta-tu."

"I think the saddle blanket is perfect," replied Kat. "Especially if you're making it yourself. The best gifts share something of the person who gives them."

"Those are wise words," said Chin thoughtfully. Then she smiled. "Now shall we go for another riding lesson?"

Kat's worry must have been obvious. For Chin quickly

added, "I will make sure that Desert Wind behaves herself."

"It's not that," Kat said. "I do want to ride. It's just..." She trailed off hopelessly.

"I understand if you do not want to talk," said Chin. "I sometimes feel that way myself. But it would be an honor to help you—if I can."

Kat sighed. "Oh, Chin, I don't know if you can help with this problem." However, she'd made up her mind. She had to talk to someone.

So Kat told her friend about the missing medallion. Of course, she didn't mention the real reason why she had to get it back. She just told Chin that the necklace had great meaning. It was something she didn't want to lose.

Kat described the medallion to Chin. And she mentioned her suspicions about Li and the astrologers.

"You may be right, Kat," the princess agreed. "After what you did yesterday, the astrologers must wonder about the source of your powers. They may have sent someone to take the medallion."

"What can I do to prove it?"

"I do not know just yet," said Chin. "But I will think of something. You and your aunt have done so much for me. I will do whatever I can to help."

She turned toward her horse. "Let us begin our lesson now. I think better when I am riding."

The girls mounted and took off at a trot.

～～

Late that afternoon, Kat returned to the room to find Jessie waiting for her.

"Did you learn anything?" she asked her aunt eagerly.

"No," admitted Jessie. "Majeed was in the observatory today. But I never got a chance to speak to him. And Sung wasn't even there."

"I didn't find out anything either," said Kat. "But I did talk to Chin. She said she'll try to think of a way to help us."

Kat sighed and began changing out of her riding clothes. She was combing her hair when Chin burst into the room.

"Kat! Lady Jessica!" she cried. "I have exciting news!"

"You found the medallion?" asked Kat, her eyes shining.

For a moment, Chin looked confused. Then understanding dawned. "Oh, forgive me, Kat. I forgot. No, I have not found it."

She rushed on. "I just came to say that you are both to attend a special dinner tonight. The Khan has ordered us to join him in celebration of my upcoming marriage."

Chin continued, "This is a great honor. The Polos and some important members of the court will also be there."

Before Kat or Jessie could respond, Chin hurried over to the trunk. "Tomorrow, at the feast celebrating the New Year, you must wear white. But tonight you should wear something colorful...something special."

Chin searched through the chest. Finally she pulled out a deep-blue dress trimmed in gold. "This will do for you, Kat," she said. Next she pulled out an emerald green dress for Jessie.

"You should have something to wear over these simple gowns," said Chin thoughtfully. "I will have a servant bring you suitable robes." She got to her feet, saying, "Now I shall leave you to get ready."

They had just finished changing when a servant appeared at their door. She carried two marvelously embroidered robes over her arm.

"Princess Cocachin sent these for you to wear," said the servant.

Kat and Jessie slipped into the beautiful robes. Then they followed the girl out the door.

Kat had expected that they would return to the hall they'd visited yesterday. Instead, they were led to another part of the palace. The room they entered was large. Yet it was much smaller than the great reception hall. Lamplight revealed a half-dozen tables surrounded by low stools. One table was raised above the rest. Behind it stood a great wooden chair.

The Polos and several others were already waiting there. Kat noted some familiar faces, including those of Sung and Majeed.

Majeed gave them a brief nod before turning back to his neighbor. But Sung hurried to their side.

"Ah, come in," he said in an oily voice. A strange smile played across his face. And one hand toyed with something at his neck.

It took Kat a moment to realize what she was seeing. Then she nearly cried out in astonishment. Sung was wearing her medallion!

CHAPTER TEN

In the Wrong Hands

K at couldn't take her eyes off the medallion. She wasn't surprised to find that Sung was behind the theft. But she was shocked that he made no effort to hide the fact. Wasn't he afraid that he'd be branded a thief?

Still smiling, Sung leaned closer. He whispered to Kat, "Let us see who has the power to do magic now!" Then he whirled about and walked off.

Kat stared after him. "Jessie!" she whispered.

"I saw," her aunt angrily replied. "And heard. It looks like you were right. Sung thinks the medallion gives him great powers." With a weak laugh, she added, "He may be in for a surprise."

"What are we going to do?" Kat hissed. "We have to get it away from him!"

Before Jessie could answer, Chin appeared. Her smile dimmed as she studied their faces. "Whatever is the matter?" she asked.

"Look," responded Kat, nodding her head toward Sung. "He's wearing my medallion."

Chin sharply drew in her breath. "This is not good," she said softly. "It is as if he is challenging you to call him a thief."

"He thinks he has my 'powers' now," said Kat bitterly.

"Even without your medallion, Sung is very powerful," Chin warned her. "It would be dangerous to call him a thief without proof."

"Jessie, suppose we showed everyone your medallion?" suggested Kat. "Surely he'd have trouble explaining where he got one just like it."

"I'd hate to risk having anything happen to it too," said Jessie doubtfully.

But Chin looked excited. "You have another medallion?" she asked.

"Yes," said Jessie. "I'm wearing a silver one."

"Hmmm," murmured Chin. "That gives me an idea. Perhaps there is a way to make Sung return the medallion without calling him a thief. I will have to catch him off guard. And you will have to trust me. Even if it seems I am doing something I should not."

Kat and Jessie exchanged a glance, then nodded. "We trust you," said Kat.

Before Chin could explain further, silence fell over the room. Kat saw that Kublai Khan had arrived. Everyone, including Kat and Jessie, bowed to the emperor.

The Khan nodded and moved to take his seat at the raised table. No one else sat until after he did.

As she settled beside Chin, Kat noted that the Polos were at the next table. In all, there were at least two dozen guests. An equal number of servants stood by to wait upon them.

The Khan himself was attended by several richly dressed men. Their noses and mouths were covered with silk scarves. Chin explained that this was to keep the emperor's food and drink completely pure. Kat recognized several of the servers as barons. The task must be considered an honor, she decided.

Servants placed metal dishes of glowing coals on each table. Then they brought out firepots. Kat had seen a smaller version of these devices in her own room. From the cover of each pot rose a pipe that looked like a small chimney. As the servants set the pots over the coals, steam began to pour out of the pipes.

Before the guests began to eat, a bowl of wine was passed around. In turn, each diner dipped his or her fingers into the wine. Then they pointed up, down, and at their own foreheads. Kat and Jessie copied the others carefully. Chin told them the guests did this to thank the heavens, the earth, and their ancestors.

With that, the meal began. The diners helped themselves to the tasty stew in the firepots. And servants brought many more dishes of rich food.

However, as delicious as the food was, the meal itself was hardly pleasant. Kat quickly realized that no one spoke unless addressed by the Khan. That meant that there was no conversation while he ate.

At last the Khan finished and turned his attention to the guests. He asked the Polos some questions about their recent travels. All three men did their best to feed his curiosity. But Marco was clearly the storyteller of the group. Kat—and everyone else in the room—sat entranced as he spoke.

When Marco finished, the Khan turned his head toward Kat and Jessie. "Lady Jessica," he said, "tell me something about England."

"I am not a gifted storyteller like Marco," replied Jessie.

"And I am afraid you would find few wonders in England. You have so many things here in China that we do not. There are no fireworks in England. Nor do we have paper money or palaces as fine and large as yours."

"That may be," said the Khan, pleased at the praise. "However, it is plain that you do have great magic in England."

At the Khan's words, Kat's eyes darted to Sung. The astrologer smiled and stroked the medallion around his neck.

Majeed, who sat nearby, glanced at Sung curiously. Obviously, he wondered about the medallion—and about Sung's behavior.

Now the Khan turned to Chin. "This feast is in your honor, princess. The entire court of Ta-tu rejoices in your upcoming marriage."

Chin smiled. "None more than myself, your highness. I am most fortunate to be chosen as a wife for Argon."

"Excellent," said Kublai Khan.

Chin nodded and continued. "I would ask a favor of you, Great Khan. One last thing to make my happiness complete."

There was a hushed gasp throughout the room. I guess the Khan isn't usually asked for favors, thought Kat.

"A favor?" repeated the Khan. "What do you mean, princess?"

"I would like to consult with your chief astrologer about my trip," said Chin. "If I may have your permission."

"Why, of course," replied the Khan. He looked toward Majeed, the astrologer who had long supported Chin's marriage to Argon.

But to everyone's surprise, the princess turned to Sung instead. "May I have your words of wisdom, Sung?" she asked. "Can you see how my trip to Persia shall unfold? Will all be well?"

The astrologer nervously fingered the medallion at his neck. Finally he found his tongue. "Here is what I see, princess," he said. "The journey shall be a challenge. But with the help of your guides, you will reach Persia without harm."

Chin bowed to the astrologer. "Thank you. I take comfort in your words."

She hesitated a moment, then added, "Forgive me for my curiosity, Sung. I noticed that you touched your medallion as you spoke. It is an interesting piece. Is it a tool for looking into the future? May I ask where you got it? Surely it is new, for I have never seen you wear it before."

Sung squirmed as though he'd like nothing better than to flee the room. However, all the diners were listening, so the astrologer was forced to answer.

"The medallion has no power, princess," he assured her. "And as to how it came to me...why, there are many marvelous things to be found in the marketplaces of Ta-tu."

"It has such unusual markings," said Chin. "And the piece seems familiar. Where have I seen such a medallion before?" she wondered aloud.

An uneasy silence settled over the room.

"Ah, I remember!" said Chin at last. "Lady Jessica, do you not have one like it?"

Jessie nodded. "See for yourself," she said. She pulled the silver medallion out from under her gown.

Chin moved closer to touch the necklace. "They are so very much alike!" she remarked. "Lady Jessica, where did you get yours?"

"It was passed down to me," said Jessie. "By my great-uncle."

"Ah!" exclaimed Chin. "So it is very dear to you. And now I recall. Did you not say that you once had a gold one as well? A match for the one that Sung wears? But you thought that the guides who robbed you took it?"

Jessie eyed Sung. "A gold one was stolen from me," she said.

Kat held back a smile. She could guess what Chin would say next. That perhaps Jessie's stolen gold medallion had ended up in the marketplace. And Sung—totally unaware—must have purchased it. Politeness would require the astrologer to return Jessie's property.

Suddenly the Khan spoke. "I would like to see this medallion."

Sung blinked in surprise at this turn of events. But he removed the necklace and passed it to the Khan.

The emperor turned the medallion over in his hands. "It is an interesting piece," he said. "Very interesting."

Sung smiled as though the Khan had just thrown out a lifeline. He glanced at Kat and Jessie. In a voice of pure honey, he said, "You must keep it, your majesty."

To Kat's horror, the Khan nodded and said, "I accept your gift."

CHAPTER ELEVEN

An Unexpected Gift

As the Khan draped the medallion around his neck, Chin leaned toward Kat. "I am so sorry," she whispered. "I had hoped to shame Sung into returning the medallion. I had no idea that the Khan would admire it."

The rest of the dinner seemed to drag on forever. Kat and Jessie could think of nothing except the medallion. It now seemed hopelessly beyond reach.

Kat noticed that Sung kept looking their way. He's probably trying to figure out how to get our other medallion, she thought. That would make him perfectly happy. Neither Jessie nor I would have our "powers," but he would. And he'd have pleased the Khan with a generous gift.

Kat was grateful when the Khan finally took his leave. This was the signal that the dinner had ended.

Chin walked back with Kat and Jessie. As they entered the room, Jessie noticed that the princess was close to tears.

"Don't be so upset, Chin," she said gently. "It's not your fault that things didn't work out."

"I said I would help you get your medallion back," replied Chin. "And I failed."

"We'll find another way," Kat assured her.

Jessie shook her head. "The Khan has many treasures. He

can't possibly remember them all. But I'm sure he doesn't leave them lying about where anyone can take them."

A miserable silence followed. Suddenly Chin gave a little start. "Perhaps not *take* them," she said. "Still, there may be a way to have the Khan *give* you your medallion."

"Why would he do that?" asked Kat.

"When the Khan is presented with a wonderful gift, he sometimes gives one in return," explained Chin. "And with your magic, you can create a truly marvelous gift."

Soon afterward, still bubbling with hope, Chin bid them good night. But Kat and Jessie were too worried to sleep. The New Year celebration was the next day. In just a few short hours, they had to come up with the perfect present.

They got out the silk hanging they had bought. It was beautiful, yet it was hardly worth a return gift from the Khan.

They searched through their belongings. They couldn't give the Khan the camera or the encyclopedia. To leave them behind might change history in some way. As for their money, that would mean little to the richest man in the land.

"What do you give someone who owns everything?" Jessie muttered. "It's pretty hard to impress him. I wish we really did have another magic trick up our sleeves."

"Another magic trick," Kat repeated. An idea slowly formed in her mind. "Jessie, I think I know what we can give the Khan! But we have to get busy right away!"

~~

Kat and Jessie dressed in the flowing white gowns that Chin had given them. It was time for the New Year celebration to begin.

They waited nervously until a servant came for them. Kat tucked the Khan's gift under her arm. "Here's hoping," she whispered to Jessie as they followed the servant out the door.

The celebration was to start outside the palace on the parade grounds. When Kat and Jessie arrived, they found thousands of people already there. From a distance, it looked as if snow had fallen over Ta-tu. But the sun was reflecting off a field of white robes, not snow.

The Khan sat on a throne high above everyone else. He too was dressed in a white robe. However, his was decorated with threads of gold.

The celebration began as thousands of elephants marched by the emperor. Each was draped in white cloth. And each carried a large, gorgeous box on its back. Kat knew the boxes held gifts for the Khan.

Following the elephants came hundreds of camels. All bore boxes and white blankets.

So many gifts, Kat thought. Suddenly she felt less sure about her own offering. How could she and Jessie ever hope to have their gift noticed?

At last the parade wound to an end. People began to pass through the front doors of the palace. The Khan, of course, went first. His many family members came close behind.

They were followed by kings and queens, princes and princesses. Kat knew that Chin must be part of this group. Next went the astrologers, barons, and other important members of the court.

For almost an hour, lines of people streamed through the palace doors. Yet thousands still remained outside, waiting to enter.

"How can the great hall hold all these people?" Kat asked

her aunt.

"I doubt if there's even enough room in the whole palace," replied Jessie. "Most of them will have to remain in the hallways. Or out here on the grounds."

"What if we don't get in?" asked Kat. "What if we can't get near the Khan?"

"Certainly you will be allowed in," said a familiar voice.

Kat and Jessie turned to find that the Polos had joined them. Marco continued, "In fact, we would be pleased if you would join us. We have a table in the great hall."

Kat and Jessie quickly accepted with thanks.

"A small repayment for what you have done," said Marco. "It is because of you that we can return home."

With the Polos as their guides, Kat and Jessie made their way to the great hall. Today the room was crowded with tables and seats placed at different heights. The Khan sat at the highest table of all. From there he could see—and be seen—clearly.

As Kat took a place at the Polos' table, Marco explained the seating arrangements. To the Khan's right sat his number-one wife. One level below them were the Khan's sons, grandsons, daughters-in-law, and granddaughters-in-law. Other family members sat still lower.

On the next level were most of the barons. Sung and Majeed also sat there. Those who were less favored simply stood or found places to sit on the floor.

Kat saw that the celebration was already under way. She watched and listened as musicians played and entertainers performed.

Finally the time came for the presentation of gifts. Kat tried to spot Chin, who was sitting at one of the raised tables.

But in the crowd, she couldn't see the princess.

Perhaps she's gone to fetch White Pearl, Kat thought. Though I don't see how she'll get her horse into this crowded hall. She may have to present the saddle blanket without White Pearl's dance.

Guest after guest approached the Khan's throne with wonderful offerings. Many gifts were made of the finest gold, silver, and jewels.

Once the Khan called to a baron, who brought forward a chest. The Khan reached in and pulled out a heavy chain of gold. This he presented to a prince who had given him nine golden carriages studded with jewels.

But that was the only time the emperor gave a gift.

Suddenly a clopping sound came from the back of the hall. All around the room, heads turned to seek an explanation.

"It's Chin!" exclaimed Kat. "And White Pearl!"

As the crowd parted, Chin led the magnificent animal forward. Across the horse's back was the saddle blanket she had

made. Its threads of gold and silver glowed as if on fire. And dozens of tiny bells tinkled as White Pearl moved. Eighty-one bells, Chin had told Kat—arranged in rows of nine each.

Chin paused at some distance from the Khan. Then she grasped the horse's lead and stepped back.

"Watch this!" Kat whispered to Jessie.

At Chin's command, White Pearl reared and danced toward the emperor. The horse stopped just in front of the Khan. As one, White Pearl and Chin bowed.

The Khan's eyes shone with pleasure. But Chin wasn't done yet.

"Great Khan, I present you with this saddle blanket that I made. And I offer you a second gift as well. One that is part of me. Please accept my horse, White Pearl. I ask that you remember me whenever you look at these gifts."

Kat choked back a cry. Chin was giving away her most precious possession!

For a moment, the hall was completely still. Silently the Khan studied the princess, whose eyes were filled with tears.

"Thank you, my child," he said at last. "I will remember you, as you say."

The Khan motioned to one of his barons and quietly issued an order. The baron nodded and stepped over to White Pearl.

But the man didn't take the horse's lead, as everyone expected. Instead, he removed the saddle blanket and carried it to the emperor.

"This is enough of a gift," said the Khan. "It will remind me of you always, Princess Cocachin."

"But I meant for you to have White Pearl as well," explained Chin.

"I understand," he answered, smiling. "But I prefer to send her with you. She will show the Persians what fine horses we raise here."

"Yes, your majesty," said Chin, a bright smile spreading across her face. "Thank you many times over."

With one last bow, the princess led her horse out of the hall.

Other gifts followed. And before long, it was time for Kat and Jessie to present theirs. They rose and made their way to the Khan.

Jessie spoke for both of them. "Please accept this simple present, your majesty," she said.

The Khan took the gift and gazed curiously at the white

silk square. Kat and Jessie had prepared their gift by sewing the silk hanging into the shape of an envelope.

"If your majesty will lift the flap...," Kat said.

The Khan did as she suggested and saw that there was something inside. He glanced at Kat, then removed the object.

No one else in the hall could see what the Khan held. But they all noted the change that came over the emperor. His eyes widened. His hands began to shake. And he mouthed words that died before they could be spoken.

Many members of the court rose in alarm. Several even dashed to the Khan's side.

But Sung was not among them. Instead, he swung upon Kat and Jessie. In an outraged roar, he demanded, "What have you done? What terrible magic have you worked to frighten the Khan?"

CHAPTER TWELVE

Picture Perfect

uards!" shouted Sung angrily. "Seize the two Englishwomen at once!"

But before the guards could move, the Khan raised his hand. "No!" he commanded. "Do not touch them!"

He glared at Sung. "I am not frightened, Sung. I am surprised that you would think your emperor is so weak!"

"Forgive me, your majesty," murmured the astrologer.

The Khan continued. "I was merely amazed. The gift is so fine, so perfect...and so magical!" He again turned his gaze to the object in his hands.

Finally the Khan handed the gift to one of the barons. The man held up a white square of paper for the crowd to see. "It is the image of the Khan," announced the baron. "He sits upon his horse, ready for the hunt."

Kat had snapped the photograph the day she'd overheard the Khan talking to the Polos.

"Such a perfect likeness!" the Khan said. "Like staring into a mirror. And this I may keep?"

"Yes, your majesty," Kat nodded.

She gave her answer calmly. However, leaving the photograph behind made both Kat and Jessie a bit nervous. In fact, it had taken some time to get Jessie to agree to doing so. They

had finally decided that the paper wouldn't last very many years. So there was little chance that one photo could ever change history.

The Khan shook his head in wonder. "I have never received such a present. Truly, this calls for a gift in return."

At once the baron who held the chest of jewels stepped to the Khan's side.

"Katherine, Lady Jessica," began the Khan. "I would like to give you a special gift." Reaching into the chest, he pulled out a gold ring with a huge stone at its center.

"This once belonged to Genghis Khan, my grandfather," he said. "I would like you to have it."

Kat bowed low. "We are honored, your majesty. However," here she hesitated for a moment. "However, we cannot accept such a valuable gift."

Before the Khan could protest, she hurried on. "Your grandfather's ring should stay here, with you and your people. If we could, we would ask for a simpler gift."

"And what might that be?" asked the Khan.

"The medallion you found so interesting," said Kat. "The one that looks like my aunt's. It would greatly please us to have it."

"Very well," said the Khan with some surprise. "Though it seems to me a small thing to offer you." He turned to a servant and issued an order.

"My servant will return with the medallion," the emperor said. "While we wait, I have a question for both of you."

"We will do our best to answer," replied Jessie.

"My question is this: Will you stay in Ta-tu and continue

to offer me your wisdom?"

Sung and Majeed looked equally upset at the Khan's words. But Jessie gave the astrologers little time to worry.

"I am sorry, your majesty. If we could honor your request, we would. But it is impossible. I have read the stars. I see that we are meant to return home."

Kat half expected an outburst from the Khan. She'd seen his anger when the Polos asked to leave.

But Kublai Khan only nodded. "I understand," he said.

Then he smiled. "I will be sorry to see you go. If I were a younger man, I would go with you. The world you come from must be very wonderful."

"It is, your majesty," said Kat. "And so is yours."

By then the servant had arrived with the medallion. At the Khan's signal, he handed the golden necklace to Kat. And with a relieved sigh, Kat hung the chain around her neck.

The gift-giving continued for some time. Then the feast and final entertainments began. Both the food and performances were more wonderful than anything Kat had yet seen. And now she could relax and enjoy them. When the celebration drew to a close, she left the hall with some sadness.

≈

"Well?" Jessie asked the next morning.

"I'm ready," said Kat with a grin. "Let's go home."

They had already said their good-byes. Chin had shed tears at the news that they were leaving.

"I will miss you, my friends," the princess had said. "I had hoped you would remain here until I set sail for Persia. But I understand that you are eager to return home."

Their next stop had been to see the Polos. They had found the three men in the great hall, waiting to speak to the Khan.

"Once more, I thank you for your part in this matter," Marco had said in a soft voice. "I will be delighted to see my homeland again."

Kat had reminded him of his promise to tell the story of his travels.

And then they had said farewell to Kublai Khan. The emperor had wanted to provide Kat and Jessie with guides, horses, and supplies. But they explained that it wouldn't be necessary. The Khan had quietly accepted the fact that such great magicians might travel in unusual ways.

Now Kat and Jessie unfolded the legs of the time machine and set it upright on the floor. Jessie put one medallion in place. Kat added the other.

"We just need some sunshine," said Kat.

They opened the doors to the outside. Bright sunlight poured over the machine. Jessie took hold of one handle, while Kat grasped the other.

The machine began to hum. In seconds a mist rose up around Kat and Jessie. Caught up in the fog, they whirled through time and space.

When the mist cleared, Kat saw that they were back in Jessie's basement. And as she'd expected, the clock indicated that only a few minutes had gone by. For almost no time passed in the present when they were gone.

"I guess we should unpack," Kat said with a happy sigh. A sudden thought struck her. "Jessie, what about my photos?"

Her aunt reached into their traveling bag. It was no longer the rich velvet it had been in China. Instead, it was once again rugged canvas.

Jessie pulled out a handful of crumbly dust. "Now we know instant photographs don't last for centuries," she said.

"I guess we should be thankful," said Kat. "Otherwise, someone might have found the one we gave to the Khan."

"That reminds me," Jessie said. "There's something else we'd better check!"

They hurried upstairs to the library. Next to Malcolm's desk, they found his well-worn copy of *The Travels of Marco Polo*.

Kat flipped through the book. Eventually she found the part that told about the Polos' years in Ta-tu.

With a relieved sigh, Kat turned to her aunt. "Marco did as we asked," she reported. "I can't find our names anywhere. He doesn't even mention meeting two female travelers."

"Nothing at all?" asked Jessie.

"Not that I can see," Kat replied. "But listen to this: He says he hasn't written of all the wonders he's seen. Because no one would believe him!"

Jessie laughed. "Do you suppose he was thinking of us when he wrote that?"

More to Explore

Have fun exploring more about life in China during the time of Marco Polo and Kublai Khan. And there are great projects for you to do too!

The Story Behind the Story

Before the thirteenth century, the Far East was a mysterious place to Europeans. Merchants bought spices, jewels, and silk from China and India. But they traded for these goods in the Middle East. They knew almost nothing about the countries from which the goods originally came.

That began to change when Kublai Khan came to power in Asia. Kublai was the leader, or Khan, of a fierce tribe called the Mongols. The Mongols eventually controlled territory from the Middle East to the Pacific Ocean—including China.

Kublai Khan wasn't simply interested in conquest. He was also eager to trade with the Western world—and to learn about it. At the same time, Europeans were growing curious about the East. Two merchants, Nicolo and Maffeo Polo, wanted to see if they could open a direct trade route with Asia. So they set off from their home in the city-state of Venice (now part of Italy) to explore the East. After years of travel, they arrived in China, where Kublai Khan eagerly greeted them.

The Polos stayed in China for several years. When they left, Kublai Khan asked them to return. They did—and this time, they brought along Nicolo's young son, Marco Polo. Marco was 17 years old when he left Venice. It would be more than 20 years before he saw his homeland again.

Marco Polo greatly admired the Khan. In turn, the Khan trusted the young man. In fact, Marco served as the Khan's rep-

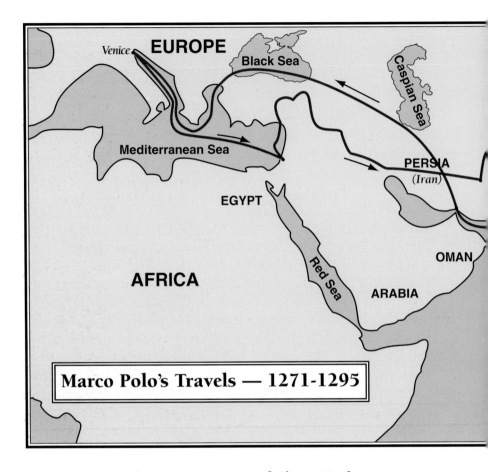

Marco Polo's Travels — 1271-1295

resentative, traveling to many parts of China. On his journeys, he saw things no European had ever seen.

Just as Kat's story describes, the Khan didn't want the Polos to leave. Finally in 1292, they were allowed to go. And they did serve as escorts for 17-year-old Princess Cocachin.

Cocachin was a real Mongolian princess. As the book tells, she was sent to Persia (now called Iran) to marry Argon, the leader of that country. An arranged marriage wouldn't have seemed at all unusual to the princess. In her day, marriage had more to do with adding to a family's power or wealth than with love.

The same was true in Europe. Women there had limited

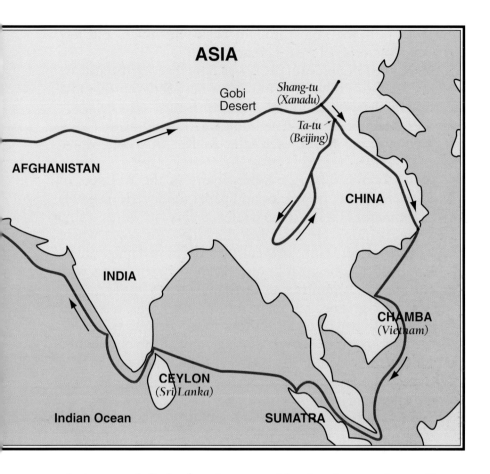

choices and little freedom outside the house. In reality, a woman and a girl such as Jessie and Kat would never have made the trip from England to China.

When Cocachin set off on her journey, 600 people went with her. Only 18 survived the long, dangerous trip from China to Persia. Among the survivors were the three Polos and the princess.

However, by the time they reached Persia, Argon himself had died. So Cocachin married Argon's son instead. This young man was said to be kinder and gentler than his father.

The Polos continued on from Persia to Venice, arriving four years after leaving China. Everyone was amazed by the strange objects the Polos brought back with them. But few believed the stories of their fantastic travels.

Marco Polo's book might never have been written if he hadn't ended up in jail. During a war between Venice and a nearby city, he was captured and imprisoned. His cellmate recorded Marco's stories. The book was known at first as *A Description of the World,* then later as *The Travels of Marco Polo.*

In his book, Marco describes many of the wonders of China, such as coal, fireworks, and paper money. He also tells of the emperor's marvelous winter palace in Ta-tu (now known as Beijing). He describes the New Year feast, where the Khan received gifts in quantities of "nine times nine." And he mentions the great knowledge of the astrologers who came from many countries to serve the Khan.

For a long time, few believed Marco Polo's tales. But slowly people began to take them more seriously. In fact, Christopher Columbus took along a copy of the book when he crossed the Atlantic in 1492. He thought it would be a useful guidebook, since he expected to arrive in Asia, not a new world.

Some historians question the accuracy of Marco's writing. He certainly left out some important details. For example, why didn't he say anything about the Great Wall of China? He surely must have seen it. He also failed to mention the Chinese use of gunpowder or tea.

But other historians agree that Marco's stories do fit known facts. So he must have seen most of the things he described.

Even for today's readers, the book offers a fascinating view of the people and places of the Eastern world. And for many centuries, Marco Polo's words were the only description that most Europeans had of these lands.

Fancy Fabric Envelope

Make a cloth envelope like the one Kat and Jessie gave to Kublai Khan. Use it to store small items such as rings, coins, or photographs. Or tuck a tiny gift inside and present it to someone special.

What you need

- Paper, pencil, ruler, and craft scissors
- Straight pins and a sewing needle
- Piece of fabric measuring at least 6" x 12". The fabric should have one finished edge (called a *selvage).*
- Sewing scissors
- Iron (Ask an adult for help or permission to use the iron by yourself.)
- Iron-on hem tape and thread to match the fabric

What you do

1. Use the diagram below to make a paper pattern. First draw an 8" x 5" rectangle. Add a triangular flap as shown. Mark the sewing lines and the two small slits shown near the flap. Then cut out your pattern.

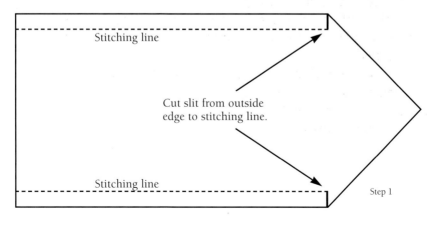

Stitching line

Cut slit from outside edge to stitching line.

Stitching line

Step 1

99

2. Pin the pattern to the fabric as shown. Cut along the outside edges of the pattern. Cut along the small slits. Then remove the pins.

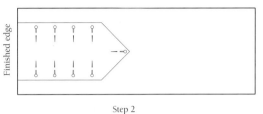

Finished edge

Step 2

3. Preheat the iron. Fold and press the pointed edges of the triangular flap as shown. The folds go toward the wrong side of the fabric.

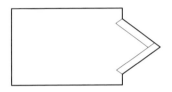

Step 3

4. Cut two 3" strips of iron-on hem tape. Iron the tape along the folded edges as shown.

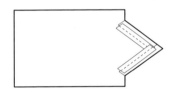

Step 4

5. Fold the fabric with the wrong side showing. Pin the edges together.

6. Using tiny stitches, sew up the two sides along the stitching lines. Be sure to knot your thread at the end of each side.

Step 5

7. Turn the envelope right side out and press the seams as shown. Then turn down the flap and press that as well. (Don't forget to turn off the iron!)

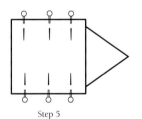

Step 7

8. You may want to decorate your envelope. You can use iron-on trims, buttons, strips of sequins, individual sequins, glitter, sew-on jewels, ribbons, fabric paint, small silk flowers, decorations cut from paper—anything you like! But be careful. If you're going to use paint or glue on the outside of your envelope, slip a piece of heavy cardboard inside first. Otherwise, the paint or glue will soak through the cloth to the back of the envelope. And if you sew trims on the outside, be sure you don't sew the envelope shut.

Chinese Cookie Treats

Make a treat that is still popular in Beijing—the Chinese city that was once known as Ta-tu. The recipe would have been different in Kublai Khan's time. Margarine didn't exist. Instead, the cookies would have been made with lard (animal fat). And at that time, Chinese kitchens didn't have ovens. The cookies would have been fried in hot oil or cooked on a flat griddle, like a pancake.

Be sure you get the help or permission of an adult to use the oven.

Sesame Cookie Puffs

What You Need

1⁄3 cup margarine	1 cup flour
1⁄2 cup sugar	1 teaspoon baking powder
1 egg	2⁄3 cup white sesame seeds

What You Do

1. Preheat oven to 350°.
2. Combine margarine, sugar, and egg in a large mixing bowl. Beat until smooth and fluffy.

Puffs (cont'd)

3. Add flour and baking powder. Mix thoroughly.
4. Using mixing spoon, stir in sesame seeds.
5. Grease cookie sheet lightly. Drop teaspoonfuls of cookie dough on cookie sheet about 1" apart.
6. Bake for 10-12 minutes. Cool on a wire rack or clean dish towel.

Makes about three dozen cookies.

Invisible Writing

Try Kat's magic trick for yourself. Use invisible ink to write a secret message to a friend.

Inks

Use any one of the following as your ink:

- Whole milk (not 2% or skim milk)
- Lemon or grapefruit juice (freshly squeezed, not from a bottle)
- A few teaspoons of sugar dissolved in warm water
- Juice of an onion (Chop some onion and set it aside until juice forms.)
- Carbonated orange soda

Writing tools

Write on white paper. Use one of the following as your pen:

- Toothpick
- Tip of a ballpoint pen that is missing its ink cartridge
- Small, fine-bristled paintbrush

Writing tips

- Use good white paper. Stationery with a little texture works best.
- Don't lose your place. If you want to pause, keep your finger at the end of the last word you wrote.
- Try mixing your invisible message with a visible one. Write a message with regular ink, leaving spaces between the lines of writing. Then write your invisible message in those spaces. Only someone who knows the secret will be able to tell that there are two messages on the page!

Reading what you write

Heat is the secret. All the inks leave traces behind. But those traces are invisible until the paper is heated. Then the invisible writing will turn brown and can be read.

Ask an adult for permission to use one of the sources of heat suggested below. Be careful—if the paper gets too hot, it can burn. And if your fingers are close to the heat, they can burn too. Remember that you must NEVER use a match or candle to read your invisible writing.

- Iron the paper with an electric iron set to medium heat. Remember to turn the iron off when you are done.

- Hold the paper over a toaster while something is toasting. Don't let the paper touch the surface of the toaster. And use a pot holder to protect your fingers!

- Hold the paper close to—but not touching—an electric light bulb.

Stardust Story Sampler

Stardust Classics books feature other heroines to believe in. Come explore with Laurel the Woodfairy and Alissa, Princess of Arcadia. Here are short selections from their books.

Selection from
LAUREL AND THE LOST TREASURE

"Company!" cried Laurel. Visitors didn't often make their way to the Dappled Woods.

"Come on, Ivy," she said to her friend. "Let's see if it's who I think it is!"

Laurel spread her wings and fluttered up to her treehouse, Ivy following.

"Aha!" Laurel cried when she reached her porch.

"Foxglove!" Ivy exclaimed.

Sitting with his feet on the porch railing was Laurel's pixie friend, Foxglove. Foxglove's visits to the Dappled Woods were usually a surprise. The pixies lived miles away in the Great Forest. Few of them had ever set foot in the fairy woods. Even Foxglove didn't visit very often.

"So what have you been doing lately, Foxglove?" asked Ivy.

"Well, I've been talking to a lot of animals in the Great Forest," explained Foxglove. "Asking what's what and where's where."

"What have you heard?" Laurel asked.

"Wonderful stories," Foxglove replied. His voice dropped to a whisper. "Stories of a long-lost treasure hidden in the

Great Forest!"

"A treasure!" gasped the others.

"Yes," said Foxglove. "Beautiful jewels and things of silver and gold."

"But whose treasure is it?" Laurel asked.

"I don't know," replied Foxglove. "Right now it doesn't seem to belong to anybody."

"Which means it's free for you to scavenge," said Laurel. "But I thought pixies were only interested in things that were useful. What do you want with jewels and silver and gold?"

Foxglove's eyes took on a strange gleam. "It's treasure, Laurel! Things no pixie has ever brought home before!" he exclaimed. "I'm known as a good scavenger. And I want it to stay that way. So I have to find this treasure before someone else does!"

"But how will you find it?"

"That's a problem," admitted Foxglove. "I've only heard hints about where it might be hidden."

He glanced at Laurel before going on. "I'm not as good at understanding animals as you are, Laurel. So I was wondering...Well, I was hoping that you'd help me out."

"You mean come with you?" Laurel asked. Her heart beat faster. "I'm not sure."

"Come on, Laurel," Foxglove begged. "It'll be a real adventure."

"I don't know," Laurel said slowly. "I'm not sure a hunt for treasure is worth going out into the Great Forest." She couldn't help thinking about how scary it sometimes was out there.

She turned to Foxglove. "You'll go even if I don't, won't you?" she asked.

The gleam in Foxglove's eyes deepened. "I have to," he said. "This is the chance of a lifetime! Why, I bet we'll end up with sacks and sacks of treasure..." He trailed off as the dream swept over him.

Laurel stared out at the peaceful Dappled Woods below her. Yes, she was a little scared of the Great Forest.

But she was also a little scared about Foxglove's hunger for this treasure. The pixie was much too caught up in the whole idea. He didn't seem to be thinking things through. Foxglove might be a great scavenger, but he needed someone else along. And as his friend, Laurel knew she was that someone.

She nodded. "All right, I'll come."

Selection from

ALISSA AND THE CASTLE GHOST

Balin closed his book and handed it to Princess Alissa.

"I've marked a spell for you to practice," the wizard said. "And now you'd better be going. Didn't you come here early this afternoon because you have to meet with Sir Drear?"

"That's right," said Alissa. "Lia and I are having a history lesson in the portrait gallery."

"Well, off with you then," said the wizard. "And keep an open mind, Alissa. You may actually learn something interesting from Sir Drear."

"I doubt it," said Alissa. "But I'll try."

The princess pulled open the door and headed down the twisting steps. Before long she had crossed the courtyard and entered the castle.

"There you are!" said Lia. "I was afraid you'd be late. And you know that makes Sir Drear cross."

"Sir Drear is always cross," said Alissa. "Do you think all stewards are like that?"

Lia laughed. "Well, running a kingdom is hard work. But I think he may be crabbier than most."

Lia got up from the bench where she'd been waiting. Together the girls walked through the arched doorway that led to the portrait gallery.

Lia walked slowly through the gallery, studying the portraits. But Alissa stopped at a window. She gazed longingly at the sunlit gardens below.

"I don't see why Sir Drear needs to show us the portraits," she said. "I've been coming here since I was small. It's not like anything ever changes. Just walls filled with paintings of people dead long ago. Every one of them sad and gloomy too."

"Maybe you haven't been looking carefully then," said Lia. "Because *he* certainly isn't sad or gloomy."

Alissa quickly joined Lia. Her friend was standing in front of a portrait of an elderly man. He was gray-haired and gray-eyed. His lips were turned up in a warm smile. And there was a friendly gleam in his eyes.

"I've never seen this portrait before!" said Alissa in surprise. She checked the nameplate on the wooden frame.

" 'Sir Grendon,' " she read. "I haven't heard of him either. And he looks like someone I'd want to know."

At the sound of footsteps, both girls moved away from the portrait. Sir Drear had arrived. Alissa and Lia watched as the tall, bony steward approached. His head was down, and he was reading some papers he had in his hands.

Alissa sighed. It was time to listen to Drear go on and on about the kingdom's history. He especially liked to talk about his own ancestors. Drear felt that every one of them had played an important part in Arcadia's past.

When he reached the girls, Sir Drear looked up. As usual, his thin lips formed a straight line across his gray face.

But instead of beginning the lesson, the steward dropped his papers. A shocked look washed over his face. Then two large spots of red appeared on his cheeks.

Slowly Drear raised a shaking hand and pointed toward Alissa. In a loud voice he cried, "What is the meaning of that?"

STARDUST CLASSICS titles are written under pseudonyms. Authors work closely with Margaret Hall, executive editor of Just Pretend.

Ms. Hall has devoted her professional career to working with and for children. She has a B.S. and an M.S. in education from the State University of New York at Geneseo. For many years, she taught as a classroom and remedial reading teacher for students from preschool through upper elementary. Ms. Hall has also served as an editor with an educational publisher and as a consultant for the Iowa State Department of Education. She has a long history as a freelance writer for the school market, authoring several children's books as well as numerous teacher resources.

KAZUHIKO SANO, illustrator of *Kat and the Emperor's Gift,* was born in Tokyo, Japan. He came to the United States to study at the Academy of Art College in San Francisco. After graduation he stayed in the U.S. and worked as a freelance illustrator. At the same time, he continued his art education, eventually earning a Master of Fine Arts degree.

Mr. Sano works full-time as an illustrator. His art was featured on a movie poster for *The Return of the Jedi* and on promotional materials for the Star Wars trilogy. He has also done paintings of dinosaurs for *Scientific American* magazine. And he is working on the design for a series of United States postal stamps to be issued in 1999.

Kazuhiko Sano is married and has two young children. He and his family live in Mill Valley, California.